Alexander Innes Shand

Fortune's wheel

A novel

Alexander Innes Shand

Fortune's wheel
A novel

ISBN/EAN: 9783337046057

Printed in Europe, USA, Canada, Australia, Japan

Cover: Foto ©Andreas Hilbeck / pixelio.de

More available books at **www.hansebooks.com**

FORTUNE'S WHEEL

"Turn, Fortune, turn thy wheel with smile or frown,
With that wild wheel we go not up or down ;

.   .   .   .

For man is man, and master of his fate."
                                        —*Æneid.*

FORTUNE'S WHEEL

A NOVEL

BY

ALEX. INNES SHAND

AUTHOR OF
'AGAINST TIME,' 'LETTERS FROM WEST IRELAND,' ETC.

IN THREE VOLUMES
VOL. I.

WILLIAM BLACKWOOD AND SONS
EDINBURGH AND LONDON
MDCCCLXXXVI

ORIGINALLY PUBLISHED IN 'BLACKWOOD'S MAGAZINE'

CONTENTS OF THE FIRST VOLUME.

FORTUNE'S WHEEL.

CHAPTER I.

A HIGHLAND HOME-COMING.

FIRST-CLASS travellers are rare in the month of June on the western and wilder section of the Great West of Scotland Railway. The season of tourists is not yet; and sportsmen seldom begin to straggle northwards before the second week of August. Through three-fourths of the year the Company must rely for dividends or debenture interest on its goods traffic — carrying cattle and sheep, herring-barrels, and wire-fencing, with miscellaneous trifles of the kind. As for Auchnadarroch station, which is situated at the head of

A

Strathoran, the station-master, metaphorically as well as physically, is one of the biggest men in the north country. Dressed in a deal of brief authority, he has the satisfaction of patronising the country-folks who travel by the trains; he is toadied in the summer by innocent Cockneys, helplessly eager for direction and advice; and he may simultaneously indulge his indolence and fussiness by managing to make an infinite ado about nothing. Save a lonely shooting-lodge or two, a couple of manses, and the residence of Glenconan, there is nothing in the shape of a gentleman's house within a radius of some score of miles; and although the "MacTavish Arms and Posting Establishment" stands within a short gunshot of the station, in those opening days of June it has barely taken down its shutters.

So it was all the stranger that, one bright afternoon in June, the station should be the scene of unwonted excitement. The platform, usually left to be cleansed by the rains and winds, was swept and garnished; the porter had taken his hands out of the pockets of his corduroys; the station-master was standing at

attention, and in close conversation with an
elderly Highlander in homespuns; while the
smoke of the train was visible in the middle-
distance, as it came sobbing and puffing up
the stiff incline. The cause of the excitement
might be explained by a carriage that had
pulled up on the shingle sweep before the
pine-built porch of the little booking-office.
It was a waggonette of teak, with a pair of
smart chestnut cobs — one and the other
strong, low, and serviceable; while the well-
set-up driver had a certain style about him
that savoured rather of the Parks and Piccadilly than of Ross-shire.

"And as I was saying to you, Mr Fergu-
son," drawled the Highlander in homespun,
"this will be a great day for Glenconan."

"I do not doubt it, Mr Ross—I do not
doubt it," replied the other, motioning away
with an affable wave of the arm the tender of
the Highlander's snuff-mull. He was excited,
and could not help showing it, though he
prided himself on the serenity of his deportment.
"We do what we can; but man's powers are
limited, and we must have resident proprietors
if we are to develop the local traffic."

Donald Ross rumpled up his shaggy eye-brows. He was a fine specimen of the elderly hillman—as tall as the station-master, and far more muscular. Hard-looking and weather-beaten, he seemed to have worked away, in a long life among the hills, all superabundant flesh from his bone and sinew. Though his Saxon was serviceable, like the cobs, he was not strong in it; he failed to catch the mean-ing of the station-master, and he struck back into his own line of thought.

"Ay, more resident gentlemen, as you were saying, will be a great thing; and it will be a great thing for Glenconan when we have one of the 'Glenconans' among us again. I'm thinking he will be turning Corryvreckan and Glengoy into deer; and 'deed these shep-herd-men are just one of the plagues of Egypt that the minister would be speaking about the former Sabbath-day."

Meanwhile the train was approaching, and at last it drew up at the platform. Three gentlemen got out of a first-class carriage. The station-master received them cap in hand, with an obsequiousness significant of the solemnity of the occasion. As for Donald, he slightly lifted his deer-stalker bonnet, and pulled shyly at a grizzled forelock; but his grey eyes gleamed with such a soft satisfaction as you may see in a friendly collie gratified by the home-coming of his master.

The foremost of the three, who naturally took the lead, was a hale veteran of about sixty or somewhat more, cast very much in the manly mould of the keeper. His dress was almost as rough, though carefully put on; but there was no possibility of mistaking him for anything but a gentleman: and if his face was beaming with excitement and good-humour, he was nevertheless the sort of man you would have been sorry to quarrel with. There was energy of purpose in the features, that were high and even harsh, as in the flash of the keen grey eyes; with a touch of sarcastic resolution about the corners of the firm mouth. His companions, who kept themselves modestly in the background, were boys in comparison. One of them might have come of age a year or two before; the other was some half-dozen years his senior.

The elderly gentleman acknowledged the salutation of the station-master with a nod, and a quick look that seemed to read the man through and dispose of him. But his greeting to Donald was cordiality itself as he held out the muscular hand, which the other evidently had expected.

"And so you're here, are you, Mr Ross, instead of upon Funachan; and this is the way you've been looking after the deer in my absence."

Donald grinned a width of welcome like the breaking of a blaze of sunshine after a thunderstorm over the waters of the neighbouring Lochconan.

"And 'deed it was very little of the deer that I was thinking of to-day, Glenconan,—though I might possibly have been speaking of them to the station-master here," he added, conscientiously. "And it's a pity but there was your piper to give you your welcome; but Peter has been palsied since the Martinmas before last—and short in the wind, moreover. And how have you been keeping, sir; and how was Miss Grace?"

"Exceedingly well, and all the better for the thought of coming home. I can answer for myself, and I can answer for her too. As for Miss Grace, you will see her here in a few days, and then she can speak for herself, which she is very well able to do. And now, Donald, lend a hand with the luggage, will you? I long to be off, and up the glen."

As for the luggage, it was light enough. The heavy baggage had been forwarded a few days before. In the twinkling of an eye the waggonette was packed; the porter, exulting over a generous tip, was looking forward to a pleasant evening in the bar of the "Mac-Tavish Arms"; and Donald sat perched beside the stylish coachman, watching the start of the impatient cobs.

There are few finer drives in the picturesque Western Highlands than that down the broad strath of the Bran and up the romantic valley of the tributary Conan. The comparatively open character of the pastoral scenery in the former valley is a fitting approach to the more gloomy grandeur of the other. Dipping into Strathoran, after some of the more savage landscapes through which you have passed in the train, you might pronounce the country almost tame. The river meanders

among gently sloping green hills, strewed
here and there with stones, and crested with
heather. From the level of the carriage-road
you seldom catch a glimpse of the towering
summits of any of the noble giants in the
background; but at the "meeting of the
waters," where the Conan joins the Bran,
the scenery changes its character altogether.
Entering the side-gorge, where the shadows
gather even at noon, we leave softness and
light for sternness and desolation. The swift
black rush of the Conan, which has been pent
for a space between beetling cliffs, pitches
itself in the exuberance of sudden release over
a brawling and foaming waterfall. The eddies
of the deep dark pool below confound themselves with the reflected blackness of interlacing fir-boughs. As for the road, it has
been roughly yet shrewdly engineered along
the sloping ledges of the cliffs that hang
between the hills and the river. It is a safe
enough ascent, for the gradients are broad
though steep, but a dangerous place to drive
down under any circumstances; for it is only
fenced on the river-side by an occasional up-
right stone in the Alpine fashion, and its

gravel is apt to be washed and mined by the side-rills flowing across it from a succession of trickling cascades.

The elder of the two young men had never visited the glen before. In silent admiration, with a rapt look in his soft hazel eyes, he hung over the side of the waggonette as it swayed slightly towards the Conan, and gazed down into the depths of the abyss. The elderly gentleman, who sat by him on the front seat, drew long breaths of profound satisfaction; and yet the very next moment you would have said that his face had slightly clouded. At least so it seemed to strike the youngest of the three, whose quick eyes, that caught everything above and below, were suddenly attracted by the other, and watched him curiously. Not for long, however. If he thought his host had an abiding care, that must only have been a foolish fancy; and what, indeed, could be more improbable?

David Moray, the lord of those barren grandeurs of Glenconan, was at last realising the cherished dream of his life. He was returning a rich man to the paternal property, which he had only visited at rare intervals since he

inherited it; and to the shootings, which had
been leased till last year to a Southern banker.
Now he might hope to end his days there in
peace, if the dregs of life would only run
kindly. He was a sportsman born: he had
come back to a paradise of sport; and though
his life had been passed in tropical climates,
he was as hale and sound of constitution as
any man of his years could hope to be.

He could be a boy still, in the light exuberance of his spirits; and nothing keeps a man
so fresh as perennial boyhood. If he had been
coming home to Glenconan, as he used to
come, for the holidays, he could hardly have
thrown himself more heartily into the happy
excitement of the hour. As the road extri-
cated itself from the bosky entanglements of
the shaggy gorges, and swept down into a
smiling stretch of mountain-meadows, he stood
up in the carriage, though sorely puzzled to
keep his feet; for the waggonette, as it dashed
downwards with locked wheels, was rocking
about like a boat among the lake billows in a
fresh north-easter. But it was not for nothing
that Moray had so often taken the Overland
route, to say nothing of weathering the Cape.

And now that he was fairly and finally home-ward-bound, in the "kent face" of each peak and ridge he saw the features of some familiar friend of his childhood.

"Fine weather to-morrow, Donald, though of course that old glass of yours is at 'stormy' as usual; for there is the cloud-belt on the sides of Funachan : had the hill been wearing his night-cap, it would have been another matter altogether. I say, Jack, do you see that purple patch on the shoulder—there, away to the right of the gap, and just over the birch-stump ?—you should have been with me the last evening I shot there with my tenant, when we found the coveys lying like stones, though they had been wild as hawks elsewhere all through the day. Please the Fates, we'll have bloodshed there in August. And when you go out for sketches, what do you think of that for a subject ?—the pool, I mean, with the grey rock, like a chapel-gable rising out of the water. And if Leslie . is looking for a spot where he may indulge himself in dreaming and poetry, that bank of bracken under the birches there ought to suit him down to the ground—if we dare to talk

of ground, indeed, in connection with any
scene so ethereal."

In the further miles of unmeasured Highland road that led on to the old house of
Glenconan, the face and spirits of its lord
and master seemed to answer to the changes
of the weather and the scenery. It was a fine
day—a very fine day; but there were a few
fleecy and drifting clouds flitting occasionally
across the heavens, and now and again some
jutting angle of. rock would cast a streak of
blackness across the brightness of the road.
So Moray's face would from time to time be
shadowed by some darker or sadder thought,
which seemed barely to touch it in passing.
But when the waggonette pulled up before
the door of the mansion, he was the kindly
Highland host, overflowing with hospitality
and natural pride in an ancestral seat, standing on a site which had been the home of his
family for generations.

The house of Glenconan was plain and
unpretending enough, and yet its surroundings gave it infinite charm. The feudal, or
rather the patriarchal keep, had been blown
up in the "'45" with certain spare powder-

casks that were embarrassing the march of the
"red soldiers," although its foundations were
still to be seen on an adjacent knoll, over-
grown with the ground-ivy struggling through
the thick beds of bracken. As for the modern mansion, as we said, it was neither impos-
ing nor very commodious; although it ran to
a considerable number of small bedrooms and
garrets, which seemed to have been elbowed
aside by the rambling passages. It was built
in the modern medieval Scottish fashion, with
a couple of receding wings, connected with the
main body or *corps de logis* by semicircular
corridors. It was whitewashed, or "harled,"
as they say in the North; and its staring and
sadly expressionless face was toned down by
neither creepers nor climbers. But then the
situation was simply enchanting. It stood
on a gentle slope, facing towards the sunny
quarter of the south-west. Before it, lawns of
the richest and softest green, watered by the
rain-storms and the perpetual flying showers,
ran down to Lochconan. And the lake lay
sparkling like a gem in its mountain-setting,
changing colours with the changing hues of
the sky, from sapphire to emerald, and from

emerald to black onyx. Around three-fourths
of its broken circumference the little loch was
girdled by swelling knolls—winding bays re-
ceded till they were lost to sight among oaks,
and pines, and the copses of weeping birches.
On the opposite shore was a wall of sheer
precipice, where a pair of peregrine falcons
had nested from time immemorial, in an
inaccessible rift far above among the rocks.
When letting the shootings, there had always
been an understanding that these old friends
of the family were to be sacred from the gun.
But the great feature of Lochconan was its
heronry, on the haunted isle of St Gilzean.
The sainted missionary, who was said to have
dipped hundreds of pagan Celts in the waters
of his blessed spring, had subsequently received the crown of martyrdom at the hands
of his ungrateful proselytes. Since then he
had been in the habit of " walking " to a surprising extent—considering that his life during his latter years had been sedentary. Not
a man in Glenconan or the adjoining parishes
would have set foot upon the island for all the
world after dusk. It may be that the silvery
forms of the birds, floating ghost-like in the

gloaming through the stems of the larches, had something to do with the perpetuation of the legend. And a pretty kind of poetry they added to the loch, in the presence of their silent, shadowy shapes, standing motionless but wide-awake in the shallows through the day, on the look-out for unwary trout or minnows.

Behind the house and the kennels the ground rose rapidly. The steep home-paddocks, where the shaggy shooting-ponies ran loose, were skirted by shrubberies of evergreens, backed up by thickets of pine; and as the heather shot up through the rough herbage, so the green of the enclosures and the lower hills was studded with rich masses of purple. Roughly traced paths, softly carpeted here and there by the thick fall of the fir-needles, wound through the columns of the firs, or lost themselves among the birch clumps and the alder thickets. Thence they emerged on the barer steeps above, where they zigzagged upwards from side to side across the rocky beds of a couple of mountain brooks—streamlets or torrents according to the weather. And each of the light rustic bridges—each tiny bit of jutting cliff projecting through the trailing

and gnarled fir-roots—seemed to open some
new and enchanting point of view up to
the cloudland that capped the confusion of
mountains.

But more than enough of description for
the time, though, if I have bored my readers,
the memories of Glenconan are my best excuse. Strolling about before dinner, Moray
did the honours of the place to his young
friends ; and if eloquent admiration be the
sincerest flattery, he had no reason to be
dissatisfied. Though the Highland air had
sharpened their appetites, he had to remind
them, more than once, that it was high time
to dress. Leslie, who was naturally rather
taciturn, said little ; but he lingered as if
loath to tear himself away from the scenes
where each changing impression seemed invariably a change for the better. As for Jack
Venables, he jumped about like a young
chamois, in the sheer exuberance of his animal spirits, at the risk of a broken neck, or, at
all events, of a sprained ankle. And his gay
exhilaration gratified the older man far more
than the self-contained appreciation of the
other. Moray had a fellow-feeling for the

headlong nature which would be doing or even suffering rather than be still.

It was to Venables that he turned more naturally during the dinner, if he showed himself more ceremoniously hospitable to Leslie. But after all, they got on very well together; and when the cloth was removed in the good old fashion, and the decanters placed on the polished mahogany, it would have been hard to find three happier gentlemen anywhere between the Solway Firth and the Shetland Isles.

"I like your dining-room, sir, almost as much as your hills," remarked Mr Venables, surveying the former serenely over a bumper of claret; "and you'll agree with me, that is saying a good deal in its favour."

Mr Moray did agree, and smiled complacently. Indeed Jack Venables could hardly have been suspected of flattery, and connoisseurs in very various styles of art might have expressed unmitigated approval. The room was unpretentious like the house—long, out of proportion to its breadth, and by no means lofty. But it had been turned into such a sylvan hall as might have suited the

retreat of a Lord of the Isles or a Lady of the
Lake. The trophies of the chase that pro-
fusely adorned the vestibule had overflowed
into the dining-room. The walls were adorned with noble stags' heads, interspersed with
those of roe-deer and grinning wild-cats. To
each was attached a brief obituary notice,
and the inscriptions dated back for a couple
of generations and more. Even tenants of
the Glenconan shootings had taken a pride in
leaving some of the choicest of their spoils
near the scenes where they had won them—
the more so that each of the sportsmen left his
name as well as a memory behind him. The
golden eagle was setting in aerial dance to the
osprey, which spread her wings in act to soar
above the sideboard; and beneath these, a
grizzled badger was snarling at an otter about
to take a header off a moss - grown ledge.
There were trout and salmon rods, and racks
for guns and rifles in the corners, and a fair
show of somewhat grim family portraits to
boot. So far, the decorations, though you
certainly could not call them commonplace,
were what might have been seen in any
Highland gentleman's halls. But then, by

way of contrast, there glittered on the sideboard a mixed service of massive and curious
plate — wine - coolers, tankards, salvers, and
epergnes, of many dates and countries, and of
the most artistic workmanship; for Moray
had a fancy that way, and his fancies had
generally been gratified. A century and a
half before, the mere rumour of so much port-
able wealth would have set all the clansmen
and caterans by the ears between Lorne and
Lochaber.

Jack Venables looked about him and went
on : " I like the silver, I must say, even more
than the stags' heads. There now ! I was sure
I should startle you both ; but you need not
look so scandalised, my dear Leslie. I'm not
altogether so covetous as you might suppose,
and a man may admire those magnificently
chased salt-cellars, for example, without having
the soul either of a pawnbroker or of a Ben-
venuto Cellini. But I like them chiefly for
all they mean. Had Glenconan lived his life
in his native glen, we should have seen nothing
on his walls save the antlers and his ancestors.
Moreover, I may venture to remark, parenthet-
ically, that I doubt whether we should have

had Lafitte like this on the table. Now stalking deer in Glenconan is grand sport in its
way; but to be content with that, we should
be born to the ambition, like Donald the
keeper. The tankards, &c., are the veritable
trophies that are worth the winning; for they
mean energy and adventure, and the excitement of success—the only things that make
life worth the living. If I know myself, I'm
nothing of a visionary: I believe in the bless-
ings of riches, and realise their anxieties too,
as much as anybody; but I should be sorry all
the same to have been born to a fortune—to
a great fortune, that is to say. Of course I
should go steadier as well as quicker if I had
a certain amount of bullion to ballast me.
Now all that silver means to me the romance
of an extremely agreeable existence. Our
Uncle Moray there has had far more than his
fair share of success and fun; and if he died
to-morrow, he has every reason to be contented. There are not many men who have
had the luck to find their way to wealth
through jungles and spice-gardens—through
cordons of Chinese junks and fleets of Malay
proas. Why, even in the way of recreation

and sport, tiger-shooting must be decidedly
preferable to deer-stalking, though it is fortunate that Donald does not hear me blas-
pheming. But hit or miss, lose or win, you
may depend upon it, Master Leslie, that excitement is everything, or pretty nearly so.
Whether we are to carry off the stakes or no,
at least we are sure of the pleasures of the
game.".

Leslie smiled good - humouredly at his
companion's long-winded rhapsody. As for
Moray, though the young man had merely
spoken in the light exhilaration of a restless
and generous spirit, had he laid himself out
to flatter and please his senior, he could hardly have succeeded more thoroughly. Moray
had himself been ardent and enthusiastic,
though with an eminently practical bent of
mind and a resolute determination of purpose.
He, too, had delighted in adventure in his
time, and the ancient fires were still glowing
in their ashes. He had loved bold speculations for their own sake—and the better that
there was a spice of danger in them. And
besides that, there was something in Venables's careless talk, in the readiness to

welcome trials which might turn to tempta-
tions, that helped to reconcile himself to his
past, and to soothe certain doubts and regrets
which had been casting their shadows across
his happiness. It pleased him, too, to remember that money meant power—that he could
give his sprightly young nephew the helping
hand he wanted; and, moreover, other vague
ideas regarding him began to take form and
consistency. The faculty of reading the
minds of other men is a gift that might be
fatal or helpful, according to circumstances or
temperaments. It is certain, at least, that it
would work a social revolution, and upset all
the existing arrangements of Providence. As
it was, Mr Venables had been rattling on in
utter heedlessness, and he never guessed how
far his chatter might have a grave influence
on his fortunes. And so the three, after a
pleasant evening, went to bed, unconscious of
all that was meant to them by that merry
meeting at Glenconan.

CHAPTER II.

A BREAK-NECK SHOOTING EXPEDITION.

WE say emphatically that June is the most
enjoyable month in the Highlands, always
supposing the weather to be conformable.
And Highland weather is so capricious, that
we may be lucky when we least expect it.
There is no shooting in June — there is no
deer-stalking.   But then the fishing of all
kinds should be in its very prime, which gives
you a pretext for enjoying the glories of the
scenery.   The trees are in the freshest rich-
ness of their foliage ; the grass is enamelled
by the early wild-flowers ; the bilberries, the
crowberries, the cranberries, and many other
berries, are putting out their brightest shoots ;
the bracken is bursting forth among the first
bells of the foxgloves,—and as both of Glenconan's guests, in their different ways, were

keen and even passionate admirers of nature,
they never found the time hang heavy on
their hands.   Moray was vexed at the arrival
of his daughter being delayed, owing to the
indisposition of the lady who was to be her
chaperon as far as Perth.   But the young men
were comparatively indifferent to the advent
of the heiress, and only expressed a decent
amount of sympathy.   To tell the truth, being
very happy as they were, they philosophically
dreaded any change in the habits of the establishment.   They did as they pleased ; they
went abroad when they liked ; and though the
dinner was a movable feast, depending on the
hour of their return, the cook might be relied
upon to come satisfactorily to time, indepen-
dently of the hands of the clock.   What with
his fishing - rod and his sketch - book, Jack
Venables could always make himself thoroughly contented.   When the trout were rising
freely, his basket filled rapidly : he could cast
a fly to the approval of Donald himself, and
under the tuition of that skilful veteran he
was rapidly being initiated in the special mys-
teries of mountain sport.   When the trout
were in no mood to take, whether in the loch,

in the lakelets, or in the streams, he seldom
cared to persevere, and fell back on his brushes
and colour-box. Excitement in one shape or
another was everything to him. He had a
rare facility of touch, a wonderful instinct for
colour; and the excitement he found in the
ever-changing lights and scenes was unfailing.
He was as happy in transferring a landscape
bathed in sunshine and flecked with shadows
to his block, as in switching the small brown
trout over his shoulder; and his pulses beat
nearly as quick to the lurid glories of a thun-
dery sunset, as when running a *Salmo ferox* on
his trolling-rod where the lake broke away
into the rapids.

As for Leslie, he took his pleasures more
contemplatively, though not more sadly. In
rallying him about his love for poetry, Moray
had touched his strength or his weakness. He
was a born poet, in perpetual sympathy with
the poetical sides of things, though, so far as
the world knew, his poetry had hitherto found
no expression. He might be born for great
things, or he might have been born to dream
away remarkable talents. In the meantime,
he could make himself placidly happy among

the scenes which brought the exhilaration of
enjoyment to his companion. No one could
deny that there was a great deal in him.
Not only had he had a distinguished career
at the university, but he could generally say
the right thing at the right moment, though
his remark might be somewhat slow of
coming: if he would hang over a repartee,
it seldom missed fire, and there was pretty
sure to be a playful snap in it when it did
come. Nevertheless, superficial observers of
natures antipathetical to his own might have
set him down for a muff or a prig, especially if
they had made his acquaintance in Highland
shooting-quarters. He rarely handled a gun
himself, though he liked to follow a shooting-
party. Made very much after the fashion of
a young Henry VIII., his somewhat bulky
and cumbrous person would have adapted
itself with difficulty to the inequalities of
difficult ground in following out an awkward
stalk; and when he did essay to throw a fly,
his line was apt to fall in coils upon the water.
Conscious of his own shortcomings, he neither
cared to correct them nor to court failure.
But he would lie on the bank for hours, watch-

ing Venables at work, his handsome features flushing over a struggle and a success; while in the intervals the thoughts that were wandering far away found ample occupation for his fertile fancy.

But a day came, in the second week of their sojourn, when the mercurial Venables felt bored, and he did not scruple to confess it. The fine weather had broken; leaden clouds lay heavy on the bosom of Lochconan, veiling the view of the opposite cliffs. The rapid fall of the barometer gave warning of a violent storm, though, as the fall had been sudden, the storm might be a passing one. As the little party were seated at breakfast, a peal of thunder seemed to burst among the chimney-pots and shake the room. Then discharge followed discharge in swift succession. The clouds were rent by the vivid flashes of the forked lightning; the rain came down in torrents, the big drops plumping in the sullen waters of the lake like showers of lead sent from the summit of a shot-tower. Then gusts of wind, sweeping in circles down from the mountains, succeeded to the preternatural calm; in places the lower half of the black cloud-curtain was lifted and blown aside, while it hung motionless as before in the shelter of the cliffs; and through gaps and rifts you caught glimpses of the hills, lighted luridly for some seconds by the fires of the lightning; while all the time the echoes were being awakened far and near, and ere one roar had died away in remote rumblings, another had come to swallow the distant mutterings. It was Byron's thunderstorm, and not much in miniature; and it was Venables, and not Leslie, who made the obvious quotation—

"And Jura answers from her misty cloud," &c.

It was a grand spectacle while the thunderstorm lasted, and Jack had every reason to be pleased with it. He strode up and down the room, returning perpetually to the windows. He rubbed his hands, and expressed unqualified admiration of the effects, till the solemnity of the disturbance oppressed even him, and he relapsed into silence in sympathy with his companions. But the thunderstorm passed away, though the rain continued to come down in torrents; and if he still paced the morning-room at intervals, he was chafing at the enforced confinement.

"You certainly are the most restless and impatient of mortals, Jack," remarked Moray, good-naturedly. "Why, young man, if you cannot bear a single day's rain, most assuredly you were never made for the Highlands."

"Not at all, sir—not at all," answered the other, laughing; "and you mistake my character altogether. I've a deal more of practical philosophy than you suppose, as I hope you may have many opportunities of remarking. If I knew we were in for a week of wet weather, Leslie himself could not take it with more serene acquiescence. But as the pigs are said to smell a gale, so I scent fine weather again, and I'm only surprised that it is so long of appearing."

Whether Venables had the weather instincts to which he pretended or not, as it happened, he was right on this occasion. The clouds did break towards evening; and moreover, there was every promise of a fine day on the morrow. He observed in the smoking-room, after dinner, and *apropos* to nothing in particular—

"I mean to go on an exploring expedition to-morrow, to Lochrosque and the Braes of Balgarroch."

"And I must say that you choose your time well," returned Moray, with a smile that was half kindly and half sarcastic. "Why, every one of the burns will be coming down in spate, and the peat-bogs will be holding the rain like so many sponges."

"And that, my dear uncle, is the very reason, or partly the reason. There will be no fishing till the rain runs off a bit; and I want exercise and excitement after the day's imprisonment. The streams will be flooded, it is true; but surely one can 'walk' or wade them somehow: and if the bogs be like sponges, as you say, why, my muscles want stretching."

"Stretched they will be, or strained or sprained: we should have to fetch you home ignominiously on the back of a shooting-pony, and then you might have a chance of practising patience through a protracted term of confinement. No, my good boy, be guided by me. Go in for a walk to-morrow, by all means, but don't attempt the innermost recesses of our Dark Continent."

But if there was one thing on which Venables prided himself, it was in sticking to a pet scheme he had originated.

"Of course, if you put your veto on it, sir, I have nothing more to say; but even if there were a dash of risk in the expedition, as there is none, I know you would be the last man to grudge me the fun of it."

"Well, well, my good boy, you must go your own way. I suppose the worst that can happen, after all, is your being knocked up after a mud-bath in a moss-pit. Only, if you do go, you must be content to take one of the gillies. I send Donald to-morrow to Dingwall after some dogs."

"And the absence of Donald is half the battle. Not that I do not appreciate his society. I never met a fellow who was better company. But Donald is as much at home among his hills as a policeman on his beat in Pall Mall; and no exploration can be possible when one is in charge of a dry-nurse. But I shall take Peter, if you will allow me. I want a man to carry a rifle."

"Take Peter, and carry a rifle? Is the boy mad? Why, Peter knows nothing of the country, and is the dullest lout on the ground. And for the rifle, it would only be so much

dead-weight, for I fancy you do not propose
to kill one of my deer in June."

"Not exactly. But I have a notion that I
may have a shot all the same,—always supposing I arrive at the end of my pilgrimage.
And as for Peter, he is a fool, and as strong
as a horse; and these are the qualities that
recommend him to me as a follower. He will
never feel the weight of the rifle, and will certainly not volunteer advice."

"Go your own way, as I said before," returned Moray, "and amuse yourself as you
like. I have too much of the Highland hospitality to put restraint on a guest, even if he
do happen to be crack-brained and a nephew
of my own. Only remember, I wash my
hands of all responsibility, and we refuse to
wait dinner."

Leslie laughed, and chimed in—

"Don't say 'we,' sir, when you talk of
dinner. I cast in my lot with Jack Venables,
always supposing he has no objection."

"Not in the least, my dear fellow—not in
the least! I should have asked you, on the
contrary, to accompany me, but I did not care
to put the screw on. With you for a com-

panion, and the worthy Peter for a beast of burden, I consider the expedition to be perfectly equipped. And whatever be the case with me, your exertions ought to reward you. There must be matter for a baker's dozen of lyrics among the mists and braes of Balgarroch."

.　　.　　.　　.　　.　　.

The pair had made an early start. Five miles of the flat had been covered on ponies, which had subsequently been hobbled and turned loose to graze. It was in a delightful sense of freedom that the young men stretched their legs, and set their faces to breast the first slopes of the hills. As for Peter, he plodded along behind, bearing the rifle, and with a game-bag slung across his shoulders, containing whisky and sherry flasks, with the materials for luncheon. Peter's ordinary calling was that of a sea-fisherman : he usually 'listed with a shooting-staff for the short shooting season ; though this year the wages that were offered by Moray had tempted him to engage at the beginning of the summer.

Venables had got himself up in a kilt, which draped his lithe figure picturesquely enough ;

and as he strode forward, although there was
a long day before them, he sprang from tussock
to tussock on the damp ground like a roebuck.
As for Leslie, a loose shooting-coat and baggy
knickerbockers half served to conceal any
superfluity of flesh.   But if his companion cut
out the running, Leslie seemed likely to stay
tolerably well ; and indeed he was no novice in
pedestrianism.   Both one and the other had
done good work in the Alps ; and Leslie,
weight and size notwithstanding, which somewhat unfitted him for crawling after deer, had
been one of the first to scale the Aiguille de
Taléfre.

"You can't possibly reproach me with pre-
mature curiosity, Master Jack ; but may I
ask now, without indiscretion, what is the
meaning of the rifle with which Peter is
encumbered ? "

"Certainly ; and I owe you many apologies
for not having anticipated your question.   But
there was something dramatically sensational
in the blind confidence with which Sense was
following the lead of Folly into the wilderness ;
and besides, the betting is a hundred to ten
that the rifle may never be brought into re-

quisition. You remember how Donald in his 'cracks' the other night turned the conversation on the goats of Balgarroch."

"Oh, that's what we're after! That's what sent us on this wild-goose—I beg pardon—on this wild-goat chase! For Donald, if I remember aright, remarked by way of postscript, that the goats were unapproachable; and the proof is, that the patriarch, if rumour is to be credited, may have been born anywhere between now and the rising of the '45."

"'Must have been born,' you mean to say. The older he is, the greater the certainty that he must be falling back by this time into his second childhood. And of course, so long as there was a deer on the hills, no one of the deer-stalkers has dreamed of going after him. Long impunity must have bred the confidence I hope to abuse."

"Say it is so. But going after a family-party of wild goats over the Braes of Balgarroch must be like looking for a lot of needles in a bundle of hay."

"I don't know that. Donald said that at this season, when the hill-grazing is fresh, they stick pretty much to the precipices to the west

of Lochrosque; and somehow, and in spite of
the Laird, I have a presentiment that we shall
have a shot before the day is over. Anyhow,
if I miss the mark, there is nobody to laugh;
for I breathed nothing of any possible intentions to Glenconan, and Peter is much too
idiotic to see anything. The secret is safe
with you, I am sure, for I know that 'Brutus
is an honourable man.'"

Brutus laughed, and silently assented. The
walking each moment was becoming more
severe, and both the men were inclined to
husband their breath.

It was lucky indeed that they were in fair
condition. Venables had scarcely turned a
hair, though he began to go more like a human
being than a chamois; and as for Leslie, if he
showed greater signs of exertion, strength and
pluck pulled him steadily through. They
plunged through yielding peat-bogs up to the
ankles, threading with many turns and pre-
cautions an intricate network of trenches and
moss-pits. They climbed hills where everything was slippery after the rain, from the
roots of the heather plants to the surfaces of
the flat stones. And shoulder to shoulder they

stemmed the strength of streams, where the
rush of the waters rose nearly to mid-thigh,
and the shifting stones in the bottom gave
treacherous foothold. The very sounds of
animated nature were either wild or melancholy, in sad harmony with the solitude of
those desolate wastes. The grouse brood
fluttered up almost under their feet as they
plunged their way through some patch of
heather. The mountain-hare started up among
the shingle and boulders, where she had been
crouching in faith in the similarity of her colour. There was the piping of the lonely little
moor-birds, and the shrill whistle of the shy
curlew; and everywhere was the plaintive
bleating of the sheep, gathered for the most
part out of sight in the sheltered corries—for
the ground they were then traversing lay beyond the limits of the deer-forest.

Both Venables and Leslie were glad enough
to see the game-bag unslung and unpacked on
the shore of Lochrosque. Bread and beef,
cheese and oatcakes, were spread on the greensward, and Peter played an admirable clasp-
knife, by way of symphony to the creditable
performance of his masters. The day was

still young, and there was time before them. Pipes and repose were veritable wisdom.

"Besides," as Venables remarked, "the worst of the work is over. I never was strong in figures, but we must have climbed 2000, or 3000, or 6000 feet, as the case may be."

Mr Venables's estimates might have been more exact, but it was evident, nevertheless, that they had attained a considerable altitude. Lochrosque was very much a counterpart of Lochconan, infinitely more gloomy, but decidedly less grand. There was not a sign of a tree about its banks; and the heather had given place to coarse grass and granite *débris*. Here and there the low flat banks were broken by weather-beaten rocks, that seemed to have been hurled by some concussion from the heights above, and to have come bounding and rolling down the slopes, till they checked themselves at the bottom of the basin; while on the opposite side to where our friends were sitting, hill rose behind hill. There was no such tremendous precipice-wall as that which frowned upon the south of Lochconan; but the hills were of granite, scantily clothed, and their garments were weather-stained and terribly tattered. Rough terraces of turf hung over clefts and abysses, and torrents had torn their way here and there from summits that were invisible from the banks of the lake. Altogether it was as break-neck a piece of Highland scenery as ever tested the head or tried the lungs and legs of an amateur.

"So these are the famous Braes of Balgarroch," remarked Leslie; "and now, I imagine, you begin to comprehend how the years of the father of the goat family should be patriarchal. If he can manage to pick up a living among these cliffs, immortality must be chiefly a question of sure-footedness."

"It looks very like it," Venables was forced to admit, as his eye ranged from height to height rather disconsolately. "I begin to have a presentiment that previous presentiments may have played me false. It is a tough bit of work, and may be a long one, on the off-chance of our getting a glimpse of the goats. Happily I took the precaution of leaving a line for 'Glenconan' in case of accidents, to say that it was just on the cards we might camp out."

"You did, did you? Happily there go two

words to that bargain, and I keep my further movements under my own control. In any case, though the days be long, we had better proceed to a survey of the country. We must cross the loch and turn that shoulder."

Peter unmoored a boat fastened under a shed, and the passage was speedily accomplished. Then the game-bag, with its reserves of food, was "cached," as they say in Western America; and hampered by nothing but the rifle, a deer-stalker's glass, and a spirit-flask, the trio commenced the climb.

Neither of the gentlemen, as has been said, were novices in the mountains, and they were by no means surprised at the piece of work cut out for them. The heights that had shut in the view from the loch-margin were merely the spurs and the shoulders of higher hills behind. Wilder and grander became the scenery as they mounted upwards—more difficult and more circuitous the walking. Sometimes the turn of a ledge brought them face to face with an insurmountable obstacle; frequently they had to descend into a ravine, that they might scramble up the opposite face, at a considerable expenditure of homespun and knee-leather. Many a time did Venables execrate the costume of the Celt in which he had draped the delicate limbs of a Saxon.

But as hunting-men will risk their necks for a bag-fox, or even a red herring, so the ostensible object of the walk was nothing to them. One was a poet, the other an artist, and artist and poet were ravished alike. The burning sun had drawn the damp from the soil, and the hills were wreathed in fantastic vapours. The very rocks were smoking and steaming, as if there were smouldering volcanic fires underneath. And now and again, when they looked down into unknown depths, they might well have been poising themselves, like Milton's Satan, on the borders of old Chaos and Eternal Night; for the billowy seas of grey shifting mists marked invisible possibil-ities of intensest desolation.

They had found breath enough to indulge in duets of sympathetic raptures, when Leslie, as the more practically-minded and thought-ful of the two, characteristically came back to the prose of the situation.

"I tell you what it is, my friend—should these mists begin to thicken, it may be more

difficult to find our way back than you seem
to fancy."

"Not a bit of it: it is only a fine-weather
haze; and the vapours will vanish with the
afternoon sunshine. There is a fine-weather
feeling in the air: just you ask Peter."

Peter, proud of being appealed to, when
the question was translated into more intel-
ligible language, answered unhesitatingly in
the affirmative. Indeed circumstances proved
afterwards that he and Venables were right;
and when they stood at last on the Pisgah-
like summit of Ben-a-Gleish, the highest hill
for a dozen of leagues around, everything was
nearly as clear below as above, and the vault
of heaven was of transparent azure.

It was high enough and bleak enough in
all conscience. They had scared more than
one pair of parent ptarmigan — the young
broods had probably scuttled for refuge beneath the stones. A pile of Cyclopean blocks,
pitched carelessly together, rose from a small
square plateau of slate and shingle. There
was a bird's-eye view of a confused panorama
of hill and valley, of black peat-moss and
bright green corrie, interspersed with rills

and streams winding their way towards lochs
and rivers. But in due time the "prospect-
glass" was supported against a walking-stick
driven into the ground, and Venables having
focussed his eye, was devoting himself to his
immediate object. Leslie had lighted a pipe,
and was looking on listlessly. He did not
believe much in the chase, but he felt amply
rewarded for the expedition——

When Venables in a stifled whisper, as if he
had been breathing the words into a telephone
of preternatural sensibility, summoned Peter
to put an eye to the glass.

"Ay, it will be them, sure enough, sir," was
the deliberate answer; "and it will not be
that difficult to make the stalk upon the
beasts, whatever."

Leslie motioned Peter aside, and took his
turn of observation. Yes, there were the
goats — the family-party; four of them were
visible, and possibly there might be more.

"And the wind is favourable," whispered
Venables, "as if the day had been arranged
for us; and nothing worse than a long circuit to make—that's to say, if they don't
shift. Once upon the top of that ridge of

rock, and they ought to be within easy range."

    .   .   .   .   .

It is an anxious moment when, after a lengthened stalk, you reach the spot you have been steering for by predetermined bearings. With Leslie and Peter following at a distance in his wake, Venables had dragged himself forward to the edge of the cliffs, and with a heart beating as if it would have burst his waistcoat - buttons, had he worn a waistcoat, he drew a hand across his eyes to brush away the streaming perspiration, — then he turned his head in the direction where the goats might be. There they were, on a bit of grassy slope, within some seventy yards of him, and the shaggy - bearded ancient, with a pair of antediluvian - looking horns, was fully exposed. A conscious sense of certainty calmed his nerves. He pulled himself together, waited to regain breath, and sent his bullet in scientifically beneath the shoulder. Leslie and Peter ran forward—too late to see the goat take a header into vacancy, while his bereaved family made a bolt round the nearest convenient corner.

"There he is—there he lies!" exclaimed the excited sportsman, having changed his place, and craned over so recklessly that his friend was fain to hold on to him by his boots. "There he is! you can just get a sight of his hoofs, kicking away still under that shelf of granite."

"I see him," said Leslie quietly, after a moment or two. "And it's only a pity you did not leave the poor beggar in peace, since there is no possibility of recovering the body."

"Perhaps not. He weighs heavy, I dare to say. I'll have the head and horns at any rate, you bet, as the Yankees say." And before Leslie could well interpose, Jack, who, with the intuition of genius, had surveyed the track, had swung himself over the edge, and was steadily though slowly descending.

Facilis descensus, &c., has passed into a proverb; and we have it on immemorial French authority, that the first step is everything, or pretty nearly so. Venables proved the truth of the former maxim, but he had reason to question the wisdom of the second. He was a youth much given over to impulses. Like

Leslie, as we have said, he was used to mountain - climbing. He had the promptitude of
pluck almost in excess—a spurt would carry
him at any time through critical danger; and
he had the confidence that came of his Alpine
experiences. He picked his way steadily
along an aerial and almost imperceptible path,
though the blood of the more phlegmatic Leslie
ran cool in watching him, and the usually imperturbable Peter tossed his arms in the air.
But his impetuosity had not counted with
contingencies, as when, after zigzagging back-
wards and forwards, all within the space of the
seventy yards, taking his final spring to the
broad shelf where the goat lay, the gravel
yielded under his feet. The rainfall of yesterday had sapped the bank; and the path he
had so deftly cleared was breached effectually.

Exaltation is invariably followed by reaction.
Had it all been comparatively smooth navigation, Jack's pluck and spirit would have
carried him through. Now he must have felt
something like Icarus, when the wax was melting on the aeronaut's pinions; and a paralysing
horror settled down upon him as he knew his
retreat to be cut off. His eyes swam; his

brain turned dizzy; and he did what was probably the wisest thing in the circumstances, and subsided on the ground with his back to the abyss.

Venables's brain was in a swimming turmoil of confusion, and had he been left to himself or to Peter, his bolt would certainly have been shot. While, as for Leslie, who had been looking on in speechless horror, his thoughts were never more clear or definite. He had weighed the circumstances in a moment, and he felt hopelessly depressed. The life and death of his companion were hanging in the balance, and his interposition would probably in no degree avail. As for the dull and respectable Peter, he was paralysed. He was more at home, at the best of times, on the deck of a herring-boat than on the hills, and was made of any stuff rather than that of a hero. All in that supreme crisis depended upon Leslie—and the thoughts that were ordinarily somewhat sluggish had answered to the spur, and were working with the velocity of lightning. It was hopeless, or almost so, to save Venables; but it was absolutely impossible to go home without him. Fancy living on to tell the tale—or conceal it,—how he had left his comrade to perish within a stone-throw of him! Leslie was a gentleman and a Christian, but scarcely a saint. He was loath to leave life at a moment's notice, with all his misdeeds and mistakes unrepented of. But his feelings of chivalry were strong, and the sense of duty was imperious. He breathed from his heart the most earnest prayer for help and mercy he had ever in his life sent up to heaven, as he stepped in his turn over the cliff and followed in the track of Venables.

He made the leap over the breach comparatively easily. It tended only too decidedly down-hill, and his ponderous initial momentum aided him. The grave question was as to getting back; but that was a question to be solved in the future.

Seldom have severed friends been reunited under more serious circumstances; and the clasp of Venables's feverish hand repaid Leslie for the risk he had run. The presence and touch of his chivalrous friend were already restoring the courage of the other. There was this difference between the two—in Venables the spirit had to fight the flesh; and he could only preserve a semblance of composure by manfully diverting his thoughts and turning his eyes away from the abyss. As for Leslie, without prying into his innermost secrets, it may be said that he could look dangers of all kinds calmly in the face. At least he gazed with less of apprehension than curiosity into the depths of the yawning chasm beneath; and before he had well exchanged a hand-shake with Venables, he was planning how they might retrace their steps. He knew he had never been so near to death, for he saw that the little gravel - platform on which they stood was already crumbling and yielding beneath their united weight. He knew there was no time to send the slow and stupid Peter to fetch help. They must save themselves, and that promptly, if they were to be saved at all. Venables was looking to him for support, encouragement, and guidance. So he proved himself true to his practical good sense—drew the whisky-flask from his pocket, and passed it to his friend.

"That's right, old fellow; take another little pull," as he watched the light come back to the eye and the colour to the cheek. "There, that will do. Wait till we are on the firm ground again before you mend your draught."

The cool promise of immediate safety did as much to restore Jack Venables's confidence as the inspiriting influences of the flask. For a few moments, at all events, he was himself again, and Leslie saw it was neck or nothing. Stooping, with infinite presence of mind and a swift sweep of his pocket-knife, he cut the beard from the shaggy billy-goat.

"We won't bother about the horns," he observed, "but we must not go back without your trophy." And that very simple remark screwed the courage of Venables to the sticking-point. It was he who gave the lead over the gap, lightly bounding up upon the ground that gave way beneath him, and so with half-a-dozen successive springs placing himself in relative safety. And then he forgot all the danger that remained, in the moments of agony that the danger of his saviour caused him. There seemed a more formidable leap than ever to be made, and Leslie had little of the lightness and *élan* which had landed Venables in comparative security. For a second or so, it appeared that he had given

himself up.   He stood as his friend had left
him, and covered his eyes with his hand.
Then he essayed to cross, but in a very
different fashion.   If he had been setting his
feet on the flags of a London pavement, he
could not have trod more firmly, though the
foothold in each instance was some scarcely
perceptible niche in the hill-face.   Will the
feet support his fourteen stone, or will they
not?   Venables's heart almost ceased to beat,
though Leslie appeared to be as composed as
ever; and in another moment, in an unaffected burst of emotional gratitude, he had
clasped his recovered friend in his arms.   Had
Leslie literally come back from the dead, he
could hardly have been more warmly welcomed.

CHAPTER III.

" YOURS FOR LIFE OR DEATH."

OUR young friends bivouacked that night among the hills on the banks of Lochrosque. With the morning's toil and the afternoon's excitement, they felt they had done at least as much as was good for them, and prudently determined to " camp out." The " shelter stone," shaped something like a Breton dolman, with its Cyclopean blocks of rugged granite, offered them very tolerable quarters. They supped lightly; they slept prosaically; they rose refreshed : so, hurrying them across the intervening bogs, we land them in sight of the house of Glenconan.

A great event had occurred in their absence. It is seldom that the master of a remote Highland residence has the chance of two thrilling sensations simultaneously; but that piece of

fortune had happened to David Moray. While
he was looking forward to a solitary dinner
and a dull evening, his dearly loved daughter
had turned up unexpectedly. Grace Moray
had a dash of the romantic in her nature, and
it pleased her to arrange a surprise for her
father. The thought of the surprise that was
in store for him beguiled the tediousness of a
slow railway journey; and as she paralysed
the self-important station-master by her unexpected arrival, so she was enchanted to be
thrown back on her own resources. It was
a dramatically appropriate stage-introduction
to her Highland home. The station-master
offered her the hospitality of his cottage while
a messenger was despatched for the paternal
waggonette. The impetuous young woman
would hear nothing of the kind. She pressed
a "machine" from the neighbouring posting-
house into her service, the horse having been
captured with some difficulty in the unenclosed
meadows where he was running loose. She
mounted the machine with her maid, leaving
the boxes to follow; and what between her
excitement over the beauties of the drive, and
her anticipations of the reception awaiting her,

her rising spirits fairly ran away with her, overflowing in rapturous ejaculations and bright
snatches of song.

She had hoped to delight her father, and
she was amply satisfied. Moray, having made
some changes in his toilet, had strolled out
upon the gravel before sitting down to dinner:
he cast an eye on the cart-track that led upwards toward Lochrosque, and turned away in
slight disappointment. Although he had lived
much alone in his time, he was naturally of
a social disposition, and would have liked to
have had dinner enlivened by a narrative of
incident. When swinging round on his heel,
before entering the hall, his eye was arrested
by a vision on the lower road—a heavy dog-
cart was pulling up the steep, the driver walking by the horse's head; and in the carriage
were fluttering female garments, while a white
pocket-handkerchief was being flown by way
of signal. He realised in a moment what had
occurred, for the road the vehicle was following led nowhere except to Glenconan. Another moment, and he was striding hatless
down the hill, as if he had started on a toe-
and-heel match against time.

Grace Moray had arranged a semi-theatrical surprise, and the meeting made a very pretty tableau. On seeing an elderly gentleman come down at the double, the intelligent horse came promptly to a standstill, and betook himself to cropping the grass by the wayside. So the young lady, in all security, could set one neatly booted foot on the wheel and take a flying leap into her father's arms. It was as well, perhaps, that her cousins did not witness the fervent embrace in which she was clasped before she was landed on the gravel. They could hardly have helped feeling envy and jealousy. As for the trim lady's-maid on the back seat and the shaggy-coated Highland driver, they looked on complacently and indifferently from their very opposite points of view.

Grace Moray had really been harmoniously as she was simply named; for there was grace in her shape and her every gesture. So it struck her father, and not for the first time, as he saw her posing on the carriage-wheel like a domestic Venus. The slight irregularity of her features only added to the piquancy of their expression; there was a laughing sweetness in her soft grey eyes, which seemed to

speak of boundless capacities of affectionate
companionship, with all the sympathetic ver-
satility that can brighten a life. With the
masses of her rich brown hair slightly ruffled
under her Spanish hat by her father's hearty
embrace, with her clear complexion heightened
by the keen mountain-air, and with her eyes
glowing with the light of health and beaming
at once with excitement and tenderness, she
was as desirable a young helpmate and mistress of an establishment as any fond father
might wish to welcome.

Circumstances change cases, and there is no
reckoning with the unexpected. A few minutes before, Moray had been longing for his
male companions; now, he saw in their prolonged absence a special interposition of Providence. His daughter, too, was very well content when she heard of the expedition that left
her to a *tête-à-tête*. The early evening passed
quickly enough : they had so much to say as
to the present and the future. But when the
shadows of the loitering Highland night began
to fall, the girl began to feel uneasy. To her
there were vague horrors and dangers in the
solitudes of those trackless hills, which she had

admired and nevertheless half shuddered at in
the fading glories of the sunset. Sitting in
the snug room, watching through the open
window the shadows thickening and widening
in the clear gloaming without, her fancy began
to work uneasily. And though she knew
nothing of the real risks, with which her father
was familiar, her growing uneasiness began to
communicate itself to him. Left to himself,
he might scarcely have given a second thought
to the absence of his young friends. Jack
Venables's note had told him it was possible.
For himself, he had run the gauntlet of serious
dangers in his time, and, with innumerable
hairbreadth escapes, had always fallen safely
on his feet. A night on the hills of Glenconan
had seemed nothing to him. Now, however,
he found himself, to his own surprise, conjur-
ing up visions of the rugged precipices above
Lochrosque, with their precarious foothold and
almost invisible goat-tracks ; and he remembered Jack Venables's headstrong pluck and
impetuous temperament. But he remembered
at the same time that Jack was in good company ; that Leslie was cool and prudent ; that
Peter, though stupid, was strong-bodied and

trustworthy; and he tried to dismiss his
doubts by saying to his daughter—

"Believe me, my dear, there is nothing
whatever to be alarmed about. Nothing worse
can possibly happen to the boys than a cool
bed among the heather, with colds in the head
to follow. In any case, we can do nothing till
the morning, for there are half-a-dozen ways
home from Lochrosque. Go quietly to bed,
and if they do not turn up for breakfast, we
shall send off a party of the gillies to meet
them, with materials to break their fast. Jack
has always an undeniable appetite; and Leslie,
though he takes it more leisurely, runs him
hard with the knife and fork."

Grace professed herself so far satisfied, and
bade her father good-night. But when he
had left her in the pretty bedroom he had
carefully seen arranged for her, her anxieties
returned, and she sent her maid away. She
threw the window open and gazed out upon
the soft Highland night. She looked at her
snow-white sheets, and contrasted them with
a couch in the heather. A bed in the heather
was all very well; on the whole, she would
have much enjoyed it herself. Couches of

fragrant heather-shoots and verdant bracken
associated themselves with all the witchery of
Scottish poetry; and what could the soul wish
better for a canopy than the star-studded
vault of the northern heavens? But then
there was another side to that picture. Those
little-known cousins of hers — one or both —
might be, and very possibly were, lying crippled or shattered at the bottom of the craigs,
with the carrion-crows and ravens for their sole
attendants. In short, when Miss Moray did
make up her mind to go to bed, it was to
anything rather than untroubled slumbers.
Youth, fatigue, and the Highland air were
lulling her into dreams, which were changing perpetually to grim phantasmagoria and
nightmares. When she rose in the early
morning, the cold bath never was more
welcome; and as it was, when she had kissed
her father's cheek, he noticed the fading of
the red Lancastrian roses that had been bloom-
ing the evening before in her face.

Meanwhile Leslie and Venables had been
still earlier risers, though for very different
reasons. Moray's shrewd knowledge of mankind had not deceived him, when he sug-

gested that Jack, under stress of privation,
would make a vigorous push for breakfast at
Glenconan. Jack might not be sentimental—
he was certainly shy as to expressing sen-
timents ; nevertheless he had made an effort
and a clutch at Leslie's hand, and said, "You
may forget, my good fellow ; but you may be
sure that I never shall. Henceforward I am
yours, for life or death."

Nor did he say much more in the course of
the long morning's walk, though possibly, like
the parrot of story, he may have thought the
more. Till at last, from one of the lower
ridges he lifted up his eyes, and saw certain
moving figures in the middle-distance of the
landscape.

"Look there, Leslie! A relief expedition
sent out in search of us. If my note was duly
delivered, for the life of me I can't understand
the Laird. I should have said he was the
very last man in the world to bother about
the off-chance of a mishap."

"It's not very likely," Leslie admitted.
"But time will show, so it's no use troubling."

"So here you are at last," shouted Moray
when they came within hail ; and both the

young men were astonished to observe that
their good-natured host and uncle was decidedly flushed and choleric. "Here you are,
after keeping the household in hot water
through half the night, and rousing some of
us from our beds in the middle of our beauty-
sleep."

Venables, although ordinarily imperturbable, was slightly taken aback for once. It
was quite a new experience of his uncle, whom,
as he flattered himself, he already knew pretty.
well. However, the next words of Mr Moray
enlightened him.

"Your cousin Grace arrived yesterday evening, and I do believe she was up and about
with daybreak."

Venables whistled in silent soliloquy. Here
was the solution of the riddle, and a wonderful instance of the power of paternal affection.
"The revolution in our ways of life is beginning with a vengeance, and in this domestic
breeze." And he added to himself with philo-
sophical resignation, "I knew that girl would
be a nuisance; and if I'm sorry, I can't say
I'm surprised." Then recollecting himself,
after congratulating her father with an *em-*

pressement rather at variance with his real
feelings, he hastened to speak of yesterday's
escape, and was eloquent in his expressions of
gratitude. He warmed as he spoke with deep
feeling, and at another time he might have
made sure of an attentive listener. But now
Moray was almost as impatient as Leslie,
who tried repeatedly to cut the story short.
Moray was eager to hasten back and relieve
his daughter's anxieties; and by common con-
sent the pair of craigsmen slackened their
pace, leaving their uncle to go forward and
announce their arrival.

The immediate upshot of the affair was to
place the meeting of the cousins on an easier
and more cordial footing than a longer acquaintance might have done. Grace had a
placid nature, or at least a naturally sweet
temperament, which went far towards keeping her quiet and calm under any circumstances. But she had a lively imagination as
well. She may have been fatigued by the
journey, and instead of sleeping soundly as
usual, she had passed a restless and anxious
night. Her feelings had been overstrung
in picturing all manner of distressing casual-

ties — follies, as she tried to assure herself,
which she had been ashamed to acknowledge to her father. But when she saw him
hurrying home unaccompanied, she had made
up her mind for the worst; and the reaction
was as great as the relief, when she knew that
her fears were unfounded. Profound thank-
fulness made her suddenly light-hearted again;
and when the younger gentlemen were passing
the gate of the short approach, her high spirits
of the day before were more buoyant for their
temporary depression.

It would have been difficult to imagine a
prettier picture than that of the bright graceful figure in the doorway of the grim old
house. And closer observation only brought
out new beauties, as both Venables and Leslie
were fain to admit. Their recollections, as
they had seen her last, were of a tall, un-
gainly, and rather forward school-girl; while
Moray, in answer to requests that had been
by no means over-urgent, had refused to show
his young friends her photograph, on the
ground that no photographer had done her
justice.

There the fond father was right. · Jack

Venables's first impression was one of unqualified admiration; and then and there he
abjured the abominable heresy that the presence of his cousin could be anything but a
gain. His second thoughts were as natural,
if less romantic; and he remembered that he
had passed the night upon the hills without
the means of paying attention to his toilet.
To tell the truth, though without the more
regular beauty of his friend's features, he was
really a very good-looking young fellow, and
need not have greatly troubled himself on
that score. There are lanky-haired men who
can never show to advantage unless they
carry a pocket-comb and a stick of cosmetic
about with them. As for Venables, he curled
slightly like a well-bred spaniel, and could
dispense with brush and comb upon occasion;
the open collar of his flannel shirt set off a
well-shaped neck to advantage, and the folds
of a well-hung kilt did justice to his active
figure; while a morning plunge in the cold
depths of Lochrosque had effaced every sign
of fatigue and over-excitement. And the
more portly Leslie, who, moreover, had never
a trace of self-consciousness about him, carried

himself naturally with an easy and high-bred air, that rose superior and indifferent to external circumstances. He would have looked the gentleman all the same, either in the solemn dignity of a Court suit and ruffles, or unpacked from the miscellaneous contents of a third-class carriage after a through-journey by oriental express from Calais to Constantinople.

First impressions go for a great deal after all, and in this case the first impressions were mutually agreeable. Of course I do not mean to hint for a moment that Miss Moray fell in love at first sight with either of her cousins, and far less with both of them. All I say is, that she saw no just cause or impediment why she should not feel for both, or either, the warmest cousinly regard. As for the young men, I should be sorry to speak so confidently. Jack Venables was impressionable, and he knew it; and falling in love at first sight, on smaller provocation, was no very novel sensation with him. While Leslie, who had no experiences of the kind, and whose processes of thought were rather sure than swift, would have been incapable, in his innocent ignorance, of analysing any similar impulse.

"Now make haste and shift yourselves, my good boys, as we say in these parts," exclaimed Moray, entirely himself again, and beaming all over with cordiality. "Grace ought never to have such a chance again of knowing what is meant by Highland appetites."

The good boys responded nobly to the appeal. The broiled trout and the kippered salmon vanished as by enchantment. Bacon followed, crisp from the fender, arranged before the glowing fire of peat that corrected the freshness of the air from the open windows. Justice was done to a certain savoury grill; and some eggs were thrown in casually to fill the chinks, before the party proceeded to trifle with oatcakes, barley scones, and preserves. Glenconan himself gave his nephews a lead across the table, making occasional casts by the sideboard and fireplace; while Grace, who was a maiden of mortal mould, kept the three gentlemen modestly in countenance. She was blessed with a healthy appetite, and felt no false scruples as to

satisfying it. But when the meal was drawing to a close, and the men were playing with
their teacups, Moray lay back in his chair and
begged Venables to resume his story.

"The fact is," he remarked in brief apology,
"that, being bothered over Grace, who was
worrying herself very foolishly, I fear I cut
you uncivilly short. You see, I saw you were
both sound in wind and limb ; and had it not
been for her, I don't think I should have
troubled about you. If Jack had gone alone
upon his madcap expedition, I don't say. But
I thought that Ralph there had him in lead-
ing-strings, and would be sure to bring him
back safe."

"I don't know about his holding me in
leading - strings," broke in Mr Venables, im-
petuously. "I fear you overrate his influence
on my foolhardiness. But I can tell you this,
that had it not been for his pluck and presence of mind—for his deliberately exposing
himself to almost inevitable destruction—I
should never have come back except upon
a stretcher, and I doubt greatly whether even
Donald would have dared to go down and pick
up the pieces. It was an ugly place "—as he

spoke, he shuddered—"and it will be long
before I forgive myself for risking such a life
as Ralph's by my own absurd and pig-headed
folly."

Leslie, embarrassed for once, was blushing
like a girl, as Moray got up to slap him on
the shoulder, with a blow that expressed the
strength of his feelings. Grace sat behind
the tea-urn with flushed face and swimming
eyes, looking from one to the other of the
young men with infinite kindness and admiration. Venables for one moment would have
given a good deal if the exciting story could
have been told the other way, and if he had
been figuring there in the *rôle* of saviour.
But he hastened to dismiss the unworthy
thought; if it did flit across his mind, the
story gained in the telling thereby. He had
the gifts of a *raconteur:* he put the situations
dramatically; he painted his own feelings of
self - abandonment and despair; he did not
even spare himself the imputations of cow-
ardice as the earth was swimming before his
eyes and his thoughts went whirling wildly
towards eternity. Then he imagined Leslie's
chivalrous resolution of self-sacrifice with the

quick intuition that belonged to him, and described the courage he had himself drawn in his extremity from contact with the stronger and more heroic temperament.

"Coming over the cliff was comparatively nothing," he concluded. "It was the sort of thing any fellow was bound to do, rather than go back alone and admit that he had not tried it; but having done so much, I believe ninety-nine out of a hundred would have only thought of how they were to get back again, and they, with the hundredth, would have been puzzled to manage it. I daresay Leslie loves his life as much as another, and yet he never gave a thought to it while mine was in peril. He was cooler when making a balustrade of himself between me and the abyss, and trying to scrape a foothold for the pair of us with his nailed shooting-boots, than he is as he sits behind his teacup, wishing himself anywhere else."

A peroration which gave Leslie the longed-for pretext for proposing an adjournment for a pipe at the kennels. Nor was Miss Moray very sorry to be left alone, in a state between smiling and crying. Seriously inclining her pretty car, like Desdemona, she had been strongly moved by Jack's animated tale, sympathising almost less with his hairbreadth escape than with his generous manner of narrating it. And on the other hand, like Rebecca in 'Ivanhoe,' Venables had been "painting a hero," and the hero had been sitting modestly beside her. She could hardly say which of her cousins had interested her most; she only knew that she felt herself strongly attracted towards both of them.

CHAPTER IV.

A PLEASANT SURPRISE.

IT seems a pity that the novelist cannot intro-
duce something like the chorus of the Greek
play, or refer the reader to explanations in an
appendix, for the succinct narration of those
preliminary details which are indispensable to
the understanding of his story. But sooner
or later the reader must be troubled with
them, and it is as well to trouble him soon
and get it over. Born to a long pedigree and
a broad inheritance of barren acres seriously
embarrassed, David Moray, as a very young
man, had been offered a chance of pushing his
fortunes in the Tropics. It was a time when
the oriental pagoda - trees bore richer fruit
than now, or at least when there were far
fewer Europeans to shake them. If there
were grander prizes to be gained, there were

greater dangers and hardships to be faced
when the adventurer turned aside from the
beaten tracks.   Resolute, persevering, and
prematurely self-reliant, young Moray was
as much tempted by the hazards as by the
prizes.   His father, with the proverbial caution of the Scot, waited till his son had a
certain experience.   Then an additional mortgage on the Glenconan estates furnished him
with a moderate capital.   Perhaps the old
gentleman might have been less freehanded
had he known more of his son's disposition.
David's daring speculations would have made
his father shudder.   The young adventurer
had taken good introductions with him, and
his pleasant ways made him powerful friends
among members of the great English firms in
the ports of China and the Malay Peninsula.
He was always a welcome guest at their
tables; he might apparently have lived in
luxurious free quarters for the duration of
his natural life.   Those of the merchants who
were sportsmen had him in special affection;
and nowhere are friendships more quickly
cemented than in sporting-parties in the solitudes of the rice-swamps or the jungles.   But

Moray was the last man in the world to " sorn,"
as they say in Scotland—that is, to sponge
upon friends. He was too full of energy, too
set upon arriving at his ends, too home-sick,
we may add—though the word scarcely ex-
presses our meaning—to linger on the circuitous road that was to lead him back to
Glenconan and a competency. Recreation in
the way of wild sports came to him naturally ;
for the rest, he never relaxed when he could
help it, save when there was nothing profitable to be done, or else to serve some definite
purpose. Those pleasant evenings over the
social board formed business as well as friendly
connections. The chats at the bivouac by the
forest-fire suggested many a topic of commercial interest. A partner of no firm in
particular, Moray became the ally and agent
of many besides the one that had trained him.
The custom regulations of China were severe ;
the contraband trade was immensely lucrative ;
European opinion was sufficiently lax on the
subject : and yet there were many gainful
affairs that were too compromising to be
lightly undertaken by the old established
houses. Not a few of these transactions were

put in Moray's way, when he had once given
guarantees of his discretion and enterprise.
No one cared to inquire how far he was
agent or principal. What was certain was,
that Fortune stood his friend; and he became notorious as much for good-luck as for
ability. Having repeatedly steered his frail
skiff in safety through the breakers, he
launched a vessel on his own account, and
mustered a crew. In other words, he finally
came out as a full-fledged merchant, with
agents at the Formosa Islands, and Singa-
pore, and sundry of the Malay towns. For
himself, he was here, there, and everywhere:
the servants—whom he well knew how to
choose, besides—could scarcely play him false,
since his visits of supervision came off when
they were least expected. So far he had the
special gift of a M. de Lesseps, that he had
the knack of establishing a friendly ascend-
ancy over native potentates. He was understood to be hand in glove with not a few of
the rajahs and sultans, and more than once
his good offices and shrewd diplomacy had
been of considerable service to the British
authorities.

He was known to be rich; and it was said
that he might have been richer, had it not
been for his occasional flying trips to Scotland. And in the days when sailing-vessels
and steamers made the circuit of the Cape,
those visits were more serious affairs than
they would be nowadays. But Moray, like
Walter Scott, was wont to say that he must
have died had he not occasionally breathed
the air off the heather; while as it was, he
had kept himself in admirable health, with an
appetite that was as sound as his heart and his
liver. During one of his furloughs, he had
buried his father in Glenconan kirkyard,
after having brightened the old man's de-
clining years by relieving the estates of the
last of their encumbrances. During another
trip, and nearly twenty years before our
story opens, he had married a wife, the
daughter of a Sussex squire, and persuaded
her to share his wandering fortunes—a step
to which her family were the more willing
to assent, that the young lady had but little
fortune of her own. The marriage was only
too happy while it lasted. To his intense
grief, poor Moray lost his wife by an epi-

demic, just as, being reclaimed and thoroughly domesticated, he had resolved to realise his property and come home. He never ceased to regret that he had not acted on the determination a year before. As it was, he threw himself into trade pursuits more energetically than ever, sending the little daughter his wife had left him to be nursed under the wing of a grand-aunt. He was relieved to be rid of the child, yet very loath to part with it—for already it had the smile and the eyes of its mother.

With the separation, his more tender feelings had it all their own way, and thenceforward he had another attraction to England. Latterly those flying home-trips of his, if they were more brief, became more frequent, especially after the opening of the Suez Canal. He had fixed the period of his final return at the age when his daughter ought to be "coming out"; and in the meantime he knew that she was in good hands. Old Miss Venables was a softhearted but sensible spinster, who had missed her vocation in not marrying. Her bright little grandniece was even more of a godsend than the very handsome annuity her brother-in-law settled on her. She devoted herself to her young charge. As Grace grew up, she engaged her an excellent governess: and the three females saw a good deal of the world in a quiet way, changing their residences from Bath to Brighton, from Clifton to Scarborough; and varying the pleasant life with an occasional excursion to the Continent.

"Grace is petted, of course," the old lady used to say; "and perhaps I spoil her a little. I'm sure I don't know; and I don't think she generally abuses her influence. But it strikes me that, though she is kind enough to talk matters over fairly, she always contrives to have her way in the end."

Which proposition Grace, if she were present, would pleasantly dispose of with smiles and kisses. Possibly being too honest to deny it, she preferred to waive the point. As for her father, he was quite satisfied with the manner of her education.

"I don't fancy you will find it very easy to spoil her; and at all events, I give you liberty to try."

And as he stroked her fair hair, and looked in her frank eyes with proud confidence, the

girl probably felt that she was put upon her
honour. At all events, any spoiling was only
skin-deep; and she grew up the most indul-
gent of domestic tyrants.

The sudden death of her aunt, which took
place about eighteen months before her ap-
pearance at Glenconan, was a sad shock. It
was somewhat softened by her finding a temporary refuge under the roof of another old
friend; for her governess had just married a
Protestant *pasteur* at Pau, where she offered
all the advantages of a home to half-a-dozen
young English ladies. There she was to await
her father's return.

The death of Miss Venables, on whom he
had devolved his paternal responsibilities, necessarily precipitated Moray's arrangements.
He set to work to wind up with characteristic
energy. As he explained to his daughter
afterwards—"The thing had to be done, and
there was little time to stand on the manner
of doing it. So I snapped a thread here, and
cut a tangle there; and if there were knots, I
untied them with my teeth or my fingers."

And when Grace remarked that she feared
he must have sacrificed something considerable

to his precipitation, he only answered, with a laugh, that if he came home with a trifle less money than he might have done, nevertheless she would be very satisfactorily tochered! "Which isn't at all, papa, what I meant, as you know."

Not even the most intimate of his mercantile connections knew anything of the exact amount of his wealth, for Moray never made unnecessary confidences. But it was certain that his only daughter, by her fortune, as by her looks and her birth, ought to be free to pick and choose among all manner of eligible suitors.

.   .   .   .   .   .

Miss Moray was generally good-humour itself—she had the happy gift of looking on the bright side of things; and indeed, with the sad exception of her recent bereavement, life had hitherto almost invariably smiled on her. But for once Miss Moray was irritable and out of sorts; and the consciousness of that unchristian phenomenon fretted her, so that her last state was far worse than the first,—so much so, that her good friend Madame Robineau had proposed a consultation with the

doctor. The bare suggestion of such an ab-
surdity did Miss Moray good, and for the first
time for several days she actually burst out
laughing.

"I don't believe I've seen a doctor since I
had the whooping-cough; and I am sure, in
my present state of health, I am quite unfit for
the interview. To face a doctor, one should
be thoroughly robust. If you had spoken of
a change of scene now, there might be something in that; and in any case, it would save
your carpets. I feel as if there were quick-
silver in my veins, and as if the chair-cushions
were catapults. Perhaps you may have remarked my restlessness," she added, innocently.

"I have indeed, my dear; and so has
Adolphe," answered Madame Robineau, so
plaintively that Grace again rippled over in
laughter. "And I do believe that a few days
at the Eaux-Chaudes will do you all the good
in the world. I don't mind giving myself
a little holiday; and I daresay Adolphe can
manage to join us on Monday, and offer us
his escort back. But I must say, my dear,
it is excessively foolish to make yourself so
unnecessarily uneasy about your father. You

know as well as I, that he troubles the doctors as little as yourself; though, to tell the truth," she added, incautiously, "I think Mr Moray has been somewhat neglectful."

For her father's most unusual silence was the grief from which Grace was suffering. As a rule, and under all circumstances, he had invariably written once a-week, although sometimes his letters might be delayed, and two or three of them delivered together. But since the latest arrival, full five weeks had elapsed; and so Miss Moray was uneasy, irritable, and indignant. She had blamed his neglect, that she might calm her anxiety; but she never endured the slightest imputation on him from another, as Madame might well have known had she reflected.

" You may be quite sure, Madame Robineau, that Mr Moray has good reasons for what he does; and for all we know to the contrary, he may be any distance away in the jungles. You speak as if he were living in Pau or Paris, where there are always letter-boxes round the corner, and telegraph stations over the way."

Madame was quick to read the unwonted storm-signals. It was rarely Grace spoke of

her father as "Mr Moray"; and, moreover,
they had been perpetually discussing during
the last fortnight all conceivable contingencies
that might have caused the delay. So she
wisely waived the question and changed the
subject, and the expedition to the Eaux-
Chaudes was duly carried out. It did not
prove much of a specific. Grace continued to
be restless and preoccupied. It was the more
disquieting in one whose natural temperament
was placid; and Madame Robineau, becoming
seriously uneasy, watched for letters almost as
eagerly as her charge.

The reverend pastor had given himself leave
from his flock on the Monday morning, arriving at the Eaux-Chaudes in time to accompany
the ladies on a drive to Gabas. They had
come back to a substantial tea; and it was
one of the consequences of Grace's feminine
upbringing that she had rather a liking for
that most objectionable meal, and usually did
it ample justice. But on this particular evening the mountain air had affected her as little
as the mountain scenery. She showed herself
as indifferent to the cutlets and the trout as
to the snow-covered summits, and the black

pine-woods, and to the green waters rushing under the rocks and through the thickets of natural box-shrubberies. And yet, as if she had not had enough of communing with nature, when she rose from the table she left her friends to a conjugal *tête-à-tête*, and went off for a solitary ramble down the valley. Though she tripped lightly away, she did not walk very far. At the first sharp turn, she stepped aside from the precipitous road, and seated herself upon a moss-cushioned stone hanging over the bed of the torrent.

I have given a very false idea of my heroine if I have represented her as in any way lacka-daisical. Few young ladies were less given to melancholy moods; though, as with all finely strung and somewhat romantic natures, many of her most enjoyable moments were tinctured with sadness. But now the dimpled chin went down into the slender hand, memory and imagination were away together upon a roving commission; and to any artist survey-ing the meditative maiden from above and behind, she might have sat for a Niobe or an image of *La Penserosa*.

I do not profess to follow her thoughts—

and indeed they were so fantastically absurd
as to be hardly worth the following. All that
can be said in extenuation is, that she had
been growing less and less like her sensible
self for a fortnight past. She had lunched
indifferently, she had starved herself at tea;
and so, like some of the solitary hermits of
the Thebaid after their severe and prolonged
fasts, she saw strange visions and she dreamed
wild dreams. Considering that Mr Moray
was "hard as nails," that the manifold experiences of many adventurous years had
proved him to bear something like a charmed
life, the tremendous situations in which she
figured him did infinite credit to the vivacity
of her imagination. Could she have counted
upon such fancies coming to her call, she
might have composed a new series of the
'Arabian Nights.' But her father's own
stories and letters from the East had sup-
plied the materials and the colouring. He
was being caught in the coils of a gigantic
anaconda, and being drawn out in ribbons
like the metal that is meant for an Armstrong
gun. He was being held to ransom by a
truculent Malay chief, who had confined him

in a cage of split bamboo, with a view to
ordering him off to execution after a course
of preparatory torture. His vessel was be-
calmed, and he was beset by pirates, with
the tints of a native crew turning unnaturally
yellow behind the boarding-nettings, while the
fleet of sweep-impelled proas was approaching
hand over hand. Struck down by the jungle-
fever or the cholera—she did not pretend to
give the precise diagnosis of the disease—he
was tossing in a grass hammock, clutching
vainly at a water-jar, while his negligent
attendant had gone sound asleep. That is
scarcely a fair outline of the commonplaces
which her fancy richly embroidered; but
something like the last of these pictures had
struck her so pathetically, that her agitation
relieved itself in stifled sobs.

And then—the mania for devising surprises
must have run in the family—and then she
was startled from her melting dream by a
hand being gently laid upon her shoulder.
While her spirit had gone fluttering from the
Pyrenees to the Tropics, it had missed the
very individual it went in search of. A
hale elderly gentleman, apparently in perfect

health and excellent spirits, having rounded
the sharp corner of the road, had paused to
take breath and admire the landscape. What
struck him most and at once, was the graceful figure in the foreground. The pose was
sad, no doubt; but when he had wiped his
forehead and rubbed his eyes, he showed
anything rather than the appropriate sympathy. On the contrary, his pleasant though
rugged features were lighted up by a sudden
illumination, as if they had caught the last
glowing reflection of the setting sun. Then
the radiance gave place to a grin of self-sat-
isfaction, as of a boy who saw his way to a
capital joke. The dignified pedestrian cast a
conscious look about him, as if to make quite
certain that he was not observed. Next balancing himself on tiptoe like an elderly faun
who had latterly fallen back upon looking
on at the forest-dances, he stepped softly
forward, as if treading among sword-blades,
and his hand had come down on the dreamer's
shoulder.

When a gentleman long past middle life
indulges in something like a practical joke, he
deserves to pay the penalty. Moray cursed

his burst of boyishness from the bottom of his heart when he saw his daughter spring up with streaming eyes, start back, and turn paler if possible than before. In her state of exaltation, and with the dash of superstition in her Highland blood, she may have fancied for the moment that she saw the *Doppelganger* of the parent whose death or sufferings she had just been bemoaning. Grace had never fainted in her life; but now she might have yielded to the weakness and sunk down, had she not been caught in a pair of strong arms. The firm grasp did more to bring her to herself than the strongest smelling-salts or sal-volatile. Like a sensible girl as she was, she called her courage to her aid, and dismissed her terrors with her idle dreams. Five minutes more, and she was the Grace who had been more or less present to him, sleeping and waking, in restless nights on the Indian Ocean and the Red Sea, as in Pullman cars between Brindisi and Paris.

"After all," he exclaimed, as they stopped for about the twentieth time in their slow saunter towards the hotel, after exchanging the fullest explanations for mutual affectionate reproaches—"after all, my penitence is already almost a thing of the past, and I hardly regret the boyish trick I played you."

"Then I am sure you ought to repent it, sir," she answered, lightly; "and you must not begin by taking advantage of my forgiving disposition."

"No, I don't think I regret it," he went on reflectively, speaking rather to himself than to her, as he returned the warm pressure of her fingers. "You see I hoped, indeed I knew, that you cared about me; but we had been so far apart and for so long. It would have been only natural had you felt nothing much warmer than friendship for a prodigal father who must have seemed strangely neglectful. Now I know better, and for the future we understand each other."

"I should think so, indeed; as if any understanding had been necessary! A prodigal father! and neglectful! What of the many letters I missed so much, that, in missing them, for the first time you made me miserable? not to speak of the presents that fell in showers on me as on Madame Robineau and dear aunt Venables. Why, sir, do you

know, we always regarded you as something
between the Good Genius who keeps the
keys of enchanted treasure-chambers, and the
mighty men of the East who never travelled
without spices and apes and peacocks."

Miss Moray's quotations had got rather
mixed, between the Magi and King Solomon
and the Queen of Sheba. But then she was
talking volubly for talking's sake, in case her
feelings should again get the better of her;
and they were standing full in sight of the
hotel windows—for which reason she did not
answer her father with an embrace, which was
the kind of coin in which he best liked to be
paid for those gifts of his. But as he had
said, they had already come to an understanding; so it did not so much matter. He
quite understood what was passing in her
mind, and changed the subject accordingly.

"Talking of scents and spices and apes, there
are no end of sandal-wood things coming round
by Gibraltar for you, and I left a monkey in
charge of my servant at the Louvre in Paris.
I picked him up from a lascar on board the
Jumna, when I struck a boat-hook into his
hide, and saved him from a watery grave.

There was something in his eyes that reminded me of you, and so I bought him for the family likeness. I don't know how the resemblance may strike you; it is rather in the expression, perhaps, than in any regularity of features."

"*Merci pour le compliment, mon père,*" said the young lady, curtseying gracefully; and when she ushered him into the sitting-room, all traces of emotion had disappeared, except perhaps for a slightly heightened complexion.

"Ah! mademoiselle then has found the physician my wife prayed her to see," remarked M. Robineau gallantly, after compliments of ceremony had been exchanged with the distinguished arrival. "And found her appetite again," he might have added; for at the inviting little supper which was quickly improvised, Grace kept her father very creditably in countenance. It was a pleasant meal, both to performers and lookers-on; nor did the party separate very early. Madame and her husband would have discreetly withdrawn, leaving the newly united relatives to their caresses and their confidences. But Moray would not hear of it. He thought his daughter

had gone through enough in the way of emotion for the time, and fancied that the best
preparation for sending her soundly to sleep
would be to amuse and distract her in the
meantime. M. Robineau, who was blessed with
an inquiring mind, was ready enough to listen
and ask leading questions. And Moray, when
fairly warmed to the work, astounded the
stay-at-home pastor with his stores of picturesque information. Grace had never seen her
father figure to such advantage; and as she
had a considerable opinion of M. Robineau's
intellect, she revelled in that gentleman's re-
spectful admiration.

" It was as if he had conjured up the *spectacle*
or the *farce*, which our principles can never
permit us," he observed to his wife in the re-
tirement of their sleeping-chamber. "It was
as a *mélange* of the travels of Marco Polo with
the extravagances of M. Jules Verne. And
what an air *grand seigneur* with it all, though
his manners are as simple as his dress was
slightly *soigné*. Ah, how *cette chère* Mees
Grace ought to be happy !"

To which Madame, who had been scarcely
less enthusiastic, sleepily but cordially assent-

ed.   For Moray's frank face, and the dignified
ease of his manner, as well as the modesty with
which he touched on any personal adventures,
were admirably fitted to ingratiate him with
the ladies.

CHAPTER V.

COUSINLY AFFECTIONS.

When M. Robineau had bid adieu to the nabob and *grand seigneur*, he expressed even more unqualified admiration than on their first acquaintance. And with good reason, for, as he gratefully remarked, " On ne pourrait pas être plus généreux." The mighty man of the East had been lavish of his gifts to the "temple" in which the worthy pastor ministered, and he had made Madame Robineau magnificent offers to induce her to devote herself for a month to his daughter. The weather was becoming too hot to make Pau a desirable place of residence ; and it was arranged that Grace was to pass a month under Madame's wing between the Baths in the mountains and Biarritz.

" Why don't you take me with you ? " she

demanded, not unnaturally. " I thought it
was agreed that we were to be inseparable for
the future."

" So I hope we shall be, my dear—till——"

" Till when ? "

" Well, till it pleases you to change your
name, Miss Moray, which seems a contingency
we are both bound to contemplate."

Miss Moray laughed, and vowed eternal
constancy or celibacy with a semi-comic seri-
ousness that by no means carried conviction.
With all her filial love, it was quite in her
mind to give her father a rival sooner or later.
Then she returned to the point in dispute, and
pressed her company with a pleading eloquence
that, as she said, should have touched a heart
of stone. But her father was obdurate, for
reasons best known to himself, and defended
his resolution with flattering sophistries.

" Were it not that we were to be so soon
reunited, my dear, nothing would induce me
to leave you. But you will know some time,
that few things are so enjoyable in life as
dallying in anticipation with pleasures that
seem certainties. Not that I have not carried
that too far occasionally. I have sat looking

at a basket of mangosteens in sultry weather,
till the moment had gone by when they could
be eaten in perfection. I have watched the
tigress playing with her cubs in the jungle,
till something suddenly scared her, and I
missed the shot."

"Your instances tell against your argument,
and your honesty is too much for you," his
daughter rejoined, very pertinently. But there
was no shaking his fixed determination, so she
could only sigh and resign herself.

After all, what had much influenced his decision was his impatience to have done with
the past and begin afresh with the future.
Grace in England would have fettered his
movements; he would always have been dis-
sipating with her or dangling after her. As it
was, he went to work indefatigably to finish
the winding up of his Eastern affairs and put
everything in train. He sought satisfactory
investments for his capital; he made a variety
of indispensable purchases, buying horses and
hill-carriages, and new batteries of guns; he
sent upholsterers to set Glenconan in order,
and engaged a suitable staff of servants. When
the princess came down to her hereditary do-

mains, she should find everything in tolerable order. He had thought of buying a house in town, and of having Glenconan entirely furnished and decorated. But the latter feat was almost impossible in the time, even had he given *carte blanche à la* Monte Christo; and he knew, besides, that if he wished to pay Grace a compliment and give her pleasure, he must leave everything to her taste, and throw the troubles of shopping on her shoulders. "What is fun to her would be misery to me," remarked this excellent parent, and the reflection brought him infinite relief.

Had Mrs Moray been still in the body, the small family-party that was to greet Grace at Glenconan might have been differently arranged. Here was a great heiress, inexperienced and unsophisticated, about to be launched on English society. "She might marry a duke," her proud father often said to himself; and indeed there seemed no just cause or impediment why she should not. Besides the money which might come in conveniently were she to marry a peer with a nominally ample rent-roll, she was well-born, well-bred, singularly winning, and accomplished to boot. For her accomplishments came to her by intuition instead of education. Like her cousin Jack, she drew and coloured with a facility that marvellously resembled genius. She would sit down to the piano and rattle you off a fantasia of her own very original conception. Brilliancy was brought in in aid of feeling; and in her intense though unconscious strength of sympathetic abstraction, she threw her whole soul into the melodious intonations. Though she had seldom crossed the Border, she would warble some plaintive Scotch air so as to bring tears to the eyes of impressionable listeners; and perhaps nothing leads on to serious love-making like mutual *abandon* in such emotional moments.

Moray knew all that as well as anybody: he was very much a man of the world, although his days had been passed in the far East; and it certainly was not his way to under-estimate the fascinations of his daughter. Yet he had deliberately chosen to throw her into the company of a couple of cousins who could scarcely be called eligible, although well aware that at any moment an accident might happen, the consequences of which it would be impossible to remedy.

For the two young gentlemen to whom the reader has already been introduced were his nephews—the one by marriage, the other by blood. Leslie, whom he liked rather than loved, was his sister's son, and proprietor of a small estate in East-Lothian. Roodholm, when the moderate jointure of the dowager Mrs Leslie was deducted, might be worth some £1200 per annum—certainly not more. But Leslie, with his many estimable qualities, was a man in whom Moray scarcely believed. As he had been heard to remark once, when touched in the liver, "That boy is doomed to die in the fulness of years and reverence, after wasting his days and frittering away his opportunities. And the best reward for his life of thoughtful benevolence would be living to attend his own funeral, and listening to the eulogies pronounced over his coffin. Yes, Master Ralph is a thoroughly good fellow, and a trustworthy; but——"

In that somewhat depreciatory estimate, perhaps Moray was mistaken, for the natures of the uncle and nephew had little in common.

Moray scarcely believed in the existence of those qualities he admired, unless their possessor was perpetually showing certificates to character in the shape of palpable evidences of visible success.

As for Jack Venables, in all essential circumstances he was infinitely less eligible than Leslie. The nephew of Moray's wife, he was the eldest son of a highly respectable Sussex rector, who was, besides, a canon of Chichester Cathedral. But the Church dignitary lived nearly up to his means, and there would be little to distribute among his numerous children. Jack might be said to have no expectations; nor had he any of those specially influential connections that almost hustle a clever young fellow uphill. If the world was his oyster, as he believed, it was for him to find the knife to open it; and he had been sorely exercised over the choice of a profession. He was in haste to arrive, and yet he longed to linger — or at least to improve each shining hour, in the way of pleasure as well as business. A life of aimless pleasure would have been intolerable to him; a life of richly repaid monotony, or of dull isolation in some

back-of-the-world colony, would have been
even worse. He would have scouted a con-
sulship and an income of £3000, had such
gifts of Providence been on the cards, since
they would have involved exile and possessing
his soul in patience through a long course of
saving. Such a career as Moray's had been,
seemed altogether different. There was perpetual excitement in it to make privations
almost pleasurable, with the chances of the
coups that carried you forward to wealth.
He honestly admired his uncle and his success; and had it occurred to the elder man to
place Venables in his shoes when he retired,
the youth would have asked nothing better of
fortune. That, however, had not occurred to
Mr Moray; and Jack, with his vague fancies
and indefinite future, seemed a singularly
impracticable subject. He might turn out
well or ill: he was the very man, according
to the Scotch saying, "to make a spoon or to
spoil a horn." For that very reason, perhaps,
Moray liked him; and, what meant more in a
man of his shrewdness, he believed in him.
He thought Jack would be well worth a helping hand, and that hand he was quite ready

to extend. So it could not have been without due consideration that he threw the impecunious but agreeable youth into familiar relations with his pretty daughter. And yet Grace's prospects caused him ceaseless anxiety; and he seldom thought of the fortune she was to inherit, without his usually equable temper being ruffled.

But whatever the future might have in store for the party at Glenconan, it was certain that they were thoroughly enjoying the present. Grace had brought delightful weather with her : balmy evenings and glorious sunsets succeeded the bright and genial days. The monkey that had been sent down from town with the heavy baggage, having shaken off the agues and shivering-fits that had oppressed him during the rains, roamed verandah and roofs like a chartered libertine, doing infinite damage to the crockery and the flower-beds when people's backs were turned. Grace had taken him in warm affection; and consequently both her cousins courted him assiduously, to the great development of the virtue of self-control. There was little affectation in that with Leslie, who was placid and long-

suffering, and whom all animals at once recognised as a friend. But it was as good as a
bit of comedy to see Jack Venables instinctively raise his hand for a cuff, or his foot for
a kick, smooth his ruffled eyebrows on second
thoughts, and fondly stroke the objectionable
animal, who probably repaid the caress with a
snarl or a snap.

And to Moray, who said nothing, though
little escaped him, "the monkey in the
family" meant a great deal. He saw that
both the cousins were, metaphorically, falling
at the feet of the heiress, though neither
might have acknowledged to himself how
much he had come to care for her. Yet he
looked on quietly, and let matters take their
course, as if the girl had been one of a dozen
daughters.

There was another individual who looked
on quietly too, seeing more than the young
lady, or his master, or anybody else suspected.
Donald Ross had vowed eternal devotion, and
had already made decided inroads on her
heart. She was frequently with him in the
outhouse, where he employed his leisure in
busking flies for the streams and lochs, or

knocking up grouse-boxes for the forthcoming shooting season. It was Donald who led her pony on expeditions into the hills, and found endless subjects of conversation with which to entertain her. He dwelt particularly on the reminiscences of those tenants of the Glen who had been shipped to the antipodes in the days of her grandfather. He revelled in the legend of the witch of Funachan, who had been notoriously in the habit of night-riding the evil-minded hill-folks in their nightmares. But she listened to him most heedfully when he would change the subject to the pair of cousins who were her constant companions. Both the old keeper and his young mistress were inclined to hero-worship; but it was hard to say which of the young men had the best of it with them. On the whole, perhaps, the stars fought in their courses for Venables. Donald would go back again and again to the adventure on the hills above Lochrosque, giving, as was only fair, the precedence in the story to Leslie.

" It's surely a sad peety, Miss Grace, that both of them were born in the South; but there's not very many of us Highland people

would have done what Mr Leslie did. I would
have thought myself twice—ay, or perhaps
more times—before I would have gone down
over that rock, even for Glenconan himself.
I would have gone, I hope ; though to me it
would have been certain destruction, for I'm
neither so young nor yet so light as I used to
be—and Mr Leslie is not that light, either.
But Peter, he will be telling me that Mr Leslie
just stepped over as if he had been setting his
foot in the ferry-boat below there. Many a
man might do that, and yet lose his head ;
but Mr Leslie was as cool—ay, as cool as a
shepherd in the drifts, or an otter in Decem-
ber. Maybe Peter is a bit of a fool ; but his
eyes are as good as another's."

So far, so well. Donald would honestly
pay the tribute of admiration demanded by
Leslie's coolness and courage. But when his
conversation turned from the saviour to the
saved, it was then that he gave way to heartfelt eloquence.

"But after all, Miss Grace, it was worth
while chancing something for Mr Venables.
He's a fine young lad that ; ay, he's a very
fine young lad. If he did lose his head a bit

on the cliff, as Peter says, it was no wonder.
If it was not that he likit the sport so well, he
would never have chanced his neck for that
ill-smelling beast of a goat. I would not have
gone up among the rocks there myself for
anything less than a hart; but the Southern
gentlemen have strange fancies. Mr Leslie is
a fine gentleman too, as Glenconan's nephew
and your cousin ought to be, Miss Grace.
But he'll sit down in the heather when we
would be after a stalk; and I've known him
drop off and go asleep, and never waken again,
till the deer was stalked and shot and to be
gralloched. But as for Mr Venables, when
once he has set eyes on his stag, he'll bristle
up and settle down to the stalk like a sleuth-
hound. It's little he'll think then of the rocks
or of the burns. I've seen him when the blood
was running down off his hands, when the
water would be draining out of the pockets of
his 'knickerbogles'; and though he may have
the sense to hearken to a whisper from me, I
would be sorry to make a sound or do anything unchancy. He's as good-humoured a
gentleman as Glenconan himself; but then he
looks as ready to get up his back as Glenconan

or a wild cat : and 'deed, were he once to set
his teeth, I wadna trust him."

Which might not be an amiable trait in Mr
Venables's character, but which nevertheless
recommended him to his cousin rather than
otherwise. Like most women with anything
in them, perhaps she inclined by preference
to a man with a spice of the devil; and in
that respect Venables resembled her father,
who was her ideal of chivalrous manhood. All
the more so that, as she often told herself,
there was something so winningly kind in
those sparkling eyes of his, when involuntarily
they seemed to soften as they met the glance
of her own.

CHAPTER VI.

AN EMBARRASSING INTERVIEW.

HAD the young men been cross-examined, they must have frankly confessed that seldom before had they been so happy as at Glenconan. The days seemed to go gliding by like the swift and silent night-flight of the owl — though that is hardly an appropriate metaphor, since the merriment was sometimes noisy enough, and they chanced to be exceptionally fortunate in sunshine. We should rather say that the joyous Sun-god had greased the wheels of his chariot, and was getting over the ground at his best pace. But their temperaments were very opposite, and thence came a strange inconsistency. Leslie, though earnest and thoughtful, was somewhat indolent, and inclined to take life lazily. So long as he was happy in the day, he left the mor-

row to look after itself. Doubtless he might
have great latent reserves of power, but it
needed some strong stimulus to make him
draw upon them; while Venables, who belonged apparently to the butterfly order of
beings, was nevertheless profoundly interested
in his own future. He was bound to make
his own way in the world; he was determined
to "arrive" sooner or later: so the most
agreeable halts in the pilgrimage were simply
sheer waste of time. He could never lie down
upon a couch of rose-leaves, without the prick
of a thorn making him inclined to spring up
again. Conscience played the part of the
metropolitan policeman, and was perpetually
bidding him get up and move on.

How far he really cared for his cousin—how
far, at least, he had fallen in love with her—
was a point that he had not carefully considered. Had he been born to a handsome
independence he would have probably paid
his court to her and proposed. But he shrank
from the nuisance of thoughts that worried;
and it was a standing trouble to him that he
must spend labour and time to attain the
easy position where he might indulge his love

and his ambition. Even if he hurried uphill by the shortest conceivable cuts, how many inestimable opportunities might be missed in the meantime! That, however, was the more reason for hastening his start, and making up his mind as to the choice of a profession. His father did not count for much in the way of an adviser; and self-reliant as he was, he felt he should be all the better for the sage counsels of experience. He had an infinite respect for the successful lord of Glenconan, and he knew that he was a favourite with his genial uncle. If he had vague fancies of some day making love to Miss Grace, it might be well that her father should be taken into his preliminary counsels, sharing the credit of his success or lightening the responsibility of failure. For Mr Venables, though thoroughly honest at heart, plumed himself on the shrewdness of his social diplomacy, and believed that you could hardly pay a more delicate compliment than in discreetly appealing for advice to a veteran's experience.

To do him justice, he had never for a moment dreamed of Moray offering him pecuniary help; and even with his ill-defined feelings as to that gentleman's heiress, his pride would have shrunk sensitively from accepting it. But Moray, as we know, viewed the matter differently, and was pleased, and at the same time somewhat curious, when Jack with unwonted solemnity requested half an hour's quiet conversation. He was anxious too, for his daughter was always in his thoughts.

"Does the young dog mean to make a proposal in form?" he asked himself. "Nothing is more natural than that he should have fallen in love; so with his coolness, I can almost fancy him capable of that. And yet I do him wrong: he is too much of a gentleman."

Jack's opening speech relieved his uncle's anxiety. The youth began abruptly, almost bluntly.

"You see, sir, it is high time I was doing something for myself; and I know nobody more capable of advising me."

"And I know nobody more willing to advise you; so go ahead, my good boy, and let me hear you state the case."

Which Jack did lucidly and succinctly. He had no money, or next to none; he saw no opening in any special direction; he might possibly get a place in some Government office; but he strongly objected to monotonous routine, and would never live contented on a moderate income—unless indeed he had failed again and again, and felt that the luck had gone fairly against him.

As he spoke, the feelings of Moray's own youth came back to his memory, and he heartily sympathised with the young fellow, who had a spirit so much like his own. Master Jack's seasonable frankness had done him more good than he fancied. But Moray was a prudent Scotchman, and did not care to commit himself hastily.

"What does your father say to it all? Of course you have spoken to him."

"My father is the best man in the world; and if he happened to be an archbishop with plenty of patronage, my father, if I assented to his wishes, would make things smooth enough. As it is, he would like me to go into the Church, and trust to treading quietly in his footsteps. But he has no livings to give away, and he never asked a favour in his life; and besides, too, I can't think it honest to mount the surplice when you don't feel the slightest vocation for the altar."

" Quite right, my boy ! " Moray ejaculated.

" Then, again, seeing that the Church is too respectable for me, I might be an artist. No objection to that, I should say, on the score of hypocrisy, for the most brilliant of artists may be as Bohemian as he likes. But though I have a decided fancy that way, I misdoubt my talent ; and unless a gentleman be a genius, he should not take to painting."

" No doubt of it," returned Moray, who, though in theory he admired artists, and would have consecrated chapels to a Titian or a Velasquez, by no means fancied the idea of a kinsman of his own failing, as he believed that Mr Venables was bound to fail.

" Well then, sir," said Jack, rather ruefully, " I come back to my starting-point,—that I have the world before me, and the question is as to the direction to steer. To think that at this very instant I may be hesitating at the *embranchement* of a dozen of paths— that it is eleven to one that I strike a wrong one, and miss the way that leads straight up to fortune ! Oh for a glimmering of your

Celtic second-sight ! Possibly Mr Ross would be the person to advise with."

Moray laughed. " If you really are standing where a dozen paths branch off, you cannot be blamed for not seeing the invisible. But so far as I can gather, you are in the middle of a mist, and are inclined to trust to your luck to group your way out of it. And there, perhaps, I, who am a Highlander, can help you, as Donald has helped you in similar difficulties ere now."

Then Mr Moray spoke out in a manner that took his nephew altogether aback. When Moray placed himself or his means at another's disposal, he was not a man to do things by halves.

" I like you, Jack, as you may have partly remarked ; and I'm an old fellow without any son of my own. Oh yes, I know I have a daughter, and I am never likely to forget it ; but so far as present appearances go, Grace will be richer than may be altogether good for her. In any case, I have enough and to spare. I don't mean to adopt you. I don't propose to treat you as my son and heir. I would not do any such injury to a spirited young man as to deprive him of all incentives to exertion. But setting you straight in some direction, and giving you a lift along, is a different affair altogether. I loved my wife well—I lost her only too soon; and I should be very happy to do something for her kinsman. The question is, What? I am sorry now that I should have disposed of my interests in the East; but I was in haste to come back and give Grace a home here. I have good friends there still, however. But, like me, you would have to begin the climb at the beginning; and money is more slowly made than it used to be."

He paused a moment, expecting very possibly that Jack would nevertheless jump at the suggestion, remembering his after-dinner speech some days before, when apostrophising the show of plate on the buffet. And had he made such an offer then, Jack would most certainly have eagerly accepted. Now the young man would have been more surprised at his own hesitation, had not his mind been illuminated by a sudden self-revelation. Brought to the point and spurred to the leap, he could not decide at once to leave his cousin behind him.   Indefinite exile meant absolute separation.   He hummed and hawed, and was sensible of a confusion which brought unwonted blushes to his comely countenance.

Nor was his embarrassment diminished by Moray's demeanour.   That gentleman had liked his nephew for his adventurous dash, and was loath to think he had been mistaken in him.   But putting himself in Jack's place, and carrying himself back to Jack's age, he knew how the launch into Eastern life would have tempted him, with the hazards that would make patience seem more than tolerable ; and pluck without perseverance seemed to him a poor quality.   Jack felt that he was being misunderstood by the man with whom, above all others, he desired to stand well.   His face grew redder ; he lost all his usual composure, and he felt the fool he knew he looked.   Moray saw that some concealment, "like a worm i' the bud," was flushing his young favourite's damask cheek, and good-naturedly made an effort to come to the rescue.

"You spoke of missing chances, my boy ; and you may miss a good one now, if you do

not give me your absolute confidence.   Whatever you may have in your mind, speak it out.
I pledge myself that I shall not think any the
worse of you."

A reckless " *tu là voulu, George Dandin,*"
feeling took possession of Venables, and carried him away.   His uncle ordered him to be
frank ; and frank he would be, with a vengeance,
come of it what might.   It was like taking a
header from the rocks into the rapids ; and
how he might come out again, who should
say ?   He had no time to reflect, and could
only act upon impulse.   " In five minutes I
may get my dismissal, and be told to pack my
traps.   Never mind : here goes—nothing venture, nothing win."   And although he stammered when he began, he was astonished to
find that his very vague ideas found persuasive
expression.

To his inexpressible delight and relief,
Moray seemed less taken aback than might
have been expected.   At all events, he listened
silently and calmly, while Jack, premising that
he intended an immediate departure from
Glenconan, went on to speak of an attach-
ment to his cousin.

"I scarcely knew my own mind, sir, till you brought me to book; but what would yesterday have been the fulfilment of my fondest dreams, means nothing to-day but a sentence of transportation: and if I dare to say as much, it is only because I may at once be put out of my misery. I think I can never be happy without Grace; I know that I am never likely to be made happy with her: so give me a word of forgiveness, and let me go in peace."

Moray stroked his moustache and bent his head in silence. Jack, who had suppressed himself after his effort of audacity, began to gain heart again and rise slowly, like a namesake-of-his-in-the-box whose springs have been temporarily flattened. Visions of an Eden with an Eve in it were opening before him. Was it possible that his uncle meant to fold him in his arms, ring for Grace, and send down the curtain with a melodramatic "Bless you, my children, and be happy"? The idea was dismissed as soon as entertained, though there was ample room left for encouragement.

"Most men in my place might have been

angry, Master Jack; and I don't know what
her mother might have said to you. But I
admire your candour; and, after all, there is
nothing criminal nor very surprising in your
feelings. Quite the contrary. . Perhaps it
was my fault that you and Grace have been
thrown so constantly together. For reasons
of my own, I have never set my heart on my
girl making what they call a great marriage.
She is sure to be well off, though she may be
less rich than you suppose. No, you needn't
protest; I don't suspect you of loving my
daughter for her 'tocher.' And in any case—
be it said without offence—she will be far more
than a match for a penniless young adventurer.
But if she did chance to take a fancy to you
—or to Leslie "—there Jack winced—" and if
you could contribute a fair share towards the
housekeeping, so that you might marry without loss of self-respect, why, I should not
stand in the way of your wishes. Not that
that advances you very far, you will say,"
seeing that Jack remained silent and non-
plussed, " since you have no means at all, and
we are merely considering ways. You don't
expect my daughter to wait for you, I pre-

sume ; but if she should happen to be disengaged when you are in a position to apply, I may make no serious objections. Mark me, young man, though I talk lightly, I mean seriously. I am sure I may trust to your honour not to compromise Grace in any way."

"I have not the slightest reason to believe that my cousin cares for me. And besides," he added, after a moment's pause, "with your permission I shall leave Glenconan to-morrow."

"Softly, softly ! You are always ice or fire. Were you to beat a retreat without sound of drum, it might make talk — or mischief—that had better be avoided. Give me your word, and stay with us for another week ; longer delay might be dangerous—for you. I take that as settled ; and I may have something to say both to you and Leslie, ere you leave—for be it understood that I am not bound to you in any way, so far as those aspirations of yours are concerned. And now to come back to your immediate concerns,— for as to these, you have more reason than before to command me."

"Believe me, I heartily appreciate your generosity, but help from you has become out of the question."

"How now, young man?" said Moray, sternly — and Venables saw how his uncle could look when he was angry,—"how now? Do you dare to tell me you are offended by language that most people would call foolish and weak?"

"God forbid, sir! How can you misunderstand me? I should have thought your own high spirit would have been more in sympathy with mine. From my uncle and very kind friend I might gratefully have accepted anything. By my frank avowal I have abandoned all hope of your help, for I can take nothing from the father of the heiress on whom I have rashly set some hopes. I said I stood at the cross-roads; and it appears I have struck into a wrong one—that is all."

"Nonsense, man!" exclaimed Moray, with extreme cordiality. "Confound the fellow!" he muttered to himself; "if he were to make love to Grace as he does to me, he would win her heart in a hand-gallop. Nonsense, man! let the night and the next day or two bring counsel. You shall stay here on your parole for another week; and before you leave for the South, we may see our way somewhat more clearly as to your future arrangements," —a prediction which proved to be true, though not precisely as Mr Moray had expected.

CHAPTER VII.

STIRRING UP OF STRIFE.

It must be owned, that after an interview of the kind, the position of any young man in Venables's place would have been somewhat distressing. He prided himself on his *savoir vivre :* he could carry off a sense of awkwardness as well as most people ; and his cousin's innocent unconsciousness helped him. Yet his manner towards her had changed, and he knew it ; and he was in perpetual terror that she might ask for an explanation. Alone with her, he was comparatively at his ease ; but he was embarrassed—very unnecessarily—when her father's eye was upon them. Where Moray trusted, he trusted implicity : if he had not trusted his nephew, he would never have spoken as he had spoken ; and although, doubtless, he may have meditated over the matter a

good deal, it was not with reference to anything passing before him. And Jack might
perhaps have felt more at his ease in one
respect, had he known that Leslie occupied his
uncle's thoughts nearly as much as himself.
But it was in his sanguine nature to jump to
conclusions ; and when certain trifling preliminary obstacles should have been smoothed
away, including the choice of a profession and
lucrative success in it, he pictured a happy
couple launched on a pleasant wedding-trip,
with wind and tide and everything in their
favour.

Yet, characteristically enough, it was not
only the thought, " Were Grace to catechise
me, what in the world should I answer ? " that
gave him a vast deal of needless anxiety.
Musing over a possible engagement, and the
minor questions that would arise out of it,
the speculations of the ridiculous young man
ran somewhat in this wise—

" I suppose if I were to marry the heiress
of Glenconan, my uncle would insist on my
taking the family name. Well, there need be
no objection to that. Venables-Moray would
sound well enough, and I might even make

such a sacrifice to love as to sink my pat-
ronymic, and style myself Moray alone. But
then he might wish us to spend the best part
of the year in Glenconan; and Grace is already
falling passionately in love with the place. I
like it myself, but I don't like the climate.
Scotland, except in the picturesqueness of the
Highlands, is only a colder and a bleaker England; and England, for that matter, is bleak
enough. After all, however, climate and
scenery are secondary points; and Grace, if
she were persuaded to love me, is just the sort
of girl to be amenable. It would be a case of
'my people shall be thy people,' &c.,—not that
I would ask her to make unreasonable sacri-
fices. And then my profession, whatever it
may be, would be reason sufficient for our
living elsewhere. Glenconan would never give
me Grace if he thought I meant to live upon
her money."

Then waking out of his Alnaschar-like
dreams, he might glance across at Leslie half
guiltily, and think how that sensible individual
would laugh at him did he guess at all that
was passing in his mind. And perhaps, on the
whole, it had hitherto been as well for Leslie

that he was profoundly ignorant of what was going on.

Then, being diverted from one train of thought, Jack's lively brain would take another turn, and towards a point that perhaps ought to have been settled in the first place. He would ask himself how far he was really in love, and whether the passion was likely to last. He knew he was extremely fond of Grace, and each day he grew fonder and more fond. But then she was a girl who deserved a husband who would worship her, and past experiences had led him to doubt his own capacity for permanent adoration. He was shrewd enough to see, that with all her spirits and brightness, if she gave herself to a man, she would give herself unreservedly, and take love so thoroughly in earnest that disappointment might wreck her life.

But, "Bah! that morbid conscientiousness of mine is the best guarantee I can offer of my constancy. I know I am tremendously fond of her now; she is just the sort of girl to gain on one, day by day; and looking at our joint future in that light, our happiness will be an incalculable quantity. In any case, there is nothing pressing, since honour ties my tongue in the meantime."

As for his uncle's offers, on more mature consideration he had pretty nearly made up his mind to accept them. " Pride is all very well up to a certain point; but pride pushed to extremes would in this case be an insult, or at all events my uncle would be apt to take it as one. I shall never forget how he flared up the other day, with a blaze in his eye like a stag breaking bay, or one of his ancestors ordering a malefactor to pit and gallows. So I suppose I may as well make up my mind to be helped; though all the same, I wish I could have managed otherwise."

Possibly that sweet spirit of resignation, that generous resolution to suffer himself to be enriched, may have brought their reward. The day before that of his intended departure, Mr Venables received a business letter. No presentiment warned him of the nature of the contents; on the contrary, he by no means liked the look of it. Though not very seriously indebted, he had run sundry "ticks" at the university and in town; and when he saw the sinister blue envelope and the stiff handwriting,—" A dun, for a thousand!" was his natural ejaculation. On tearing it open, evil omens seemed to thicken. The communication was dated from Lincoln's-Inn-Fields, and signed by an unknown firm of lawyers. With a very wry face he began to run his eye over it, and this is what Mr Venables read :—

" DEAR SIR,—We have the honour of informing you that, under the testamentary dispositions of the late Mr Isaac Philpotts, of 790 Wimpole Street, and of Brick Court, Temple, you become entitled to the amount of £10,000, free of legacy duty. As the personality of our deceased client is chiefly invested in consols, there need be no delay in realising it.

" We shall either transfer the sum as invested at the current prices of the day, or expect your instructions as to manner of payment.

" Annexed receive an extract from the will of our late client.—And we have the honour to remain your obedient servants,

" COX, GRINDLEY, & GROPER."

Extract from Will of the late Isaac Philpotts, Esq., Q.C.

"Also I leave and bequeath to John Venables, eldest son of the Rev. Cyril Venables, of Oakholm Rectory, Sussex, the sum of ten thousand pounds, free of legacy duty. And I desire it to be understood that I bequeath the said sum in memory of early and affectionate intimacy with an old school and college companion, believing that I shall best gratify my friend by assuring a moderate provision to his eldest son."

Jack read, and rubbed his eyes. His first idea was, that he was the victim of a heartless and aggravating hoax. On second thoughts, that seemed even more improbable than the marvellous piece of good-luck that had befallen him at a most critical moment. Though he had never seen Mr Philpotts in the flesh, he had often heard his father speak of him as an able and eccentric old man, who had made a figure and a fortune as a parliamentary counsel, and who, in the bustle of his busy professional life, had altogether ignored early associations.

" Anyhow," as Jack remarked, gratefully and philosophically, " his eccentricity, were it madness, had a pleasant method about it ; and if any disappointed relatives should dispute the will, this judicious legacy should be proof of sanity."

He was a free-handed young fellow as ever lived ; and of all the vices that grow upon us with age, least of all was he contaminated by that of avarice. Yet it was a strange proof of the dangerous power of gold, that, on calmly realising the news, he found they almost intoxicated him. He had read his letter on the gravel-sweep in front of the house, and he started. off for a walk, or rather a run, through the shrubberies. His lungs expanded with a sense of his good fortune—with a feeling that the legacy was the sign of a prosperous future. He left the shrubberies and climbed the hill, jumping from rock to rock and on to slippery stones, while his feet seemed to be winged like those of the feather-footed Mercury, who, by the way, was the Mammon of pagan mythology. He confounded the piece of good fortune with his personal deserts, and respected Providence for having so seasonably smiled on him. In the new-born feeling of independence, he might cordially accept the offer he had hitherto hesitated over. He would decline his uncle's money, but gratefully accept his uncle's help. He might trade upon his energy and talents, in the assurance of speedy returns; and, with a modest competency but magnificent reversions, might mate with any gentlewoman of average position, even were she his pretty and well-dowered cousin of Glenconan. And the thought brought him back to the prosaic fact, that it would be but kind and civil promptly to communicate the contents of the despatch to the relatives who were to be still nearer and dearer.

He was a good fellow, though rather feather-brained as yet; and want of liberality, as we have said, was not his failing, though he seemed as keenly set upon the quest of gold as any of the Argonauts. As it happened, he had the purse in his pocket that was fairly well-filled for his journey. Peter, the stupid gillie, had the good-luck to cross his path as he came bounding housewards from the hill like a roebuck.

" Ah, Peter, my man, you know I am going

South in a day or two; here's a trifle in re-
membrance of that bit of work of ours on
Lochrosque."

Indeed his prodigality needed some excuse,
and tears came to Peter's eye and his voice
trembled as he thanked the generous young
Saxon gentleman for a sum which meant the
ease and happiness of next winter to the wife
and bairns on Loch Hourn. As for Jack himself, he was richly rewarded: it was a new
sensation to know that money-giving could
bring so much pleasure. He vowed that he
would lay the lesson to heart, and soon he
found another occasion of practising it. It was
only turning aside for a dozen of paces or so,
and he came upon Donald Ross hammering
away industriously at grouse-boxes. Forth
came the *portemonnaie* again, and the head-
keeper was gratified with a proportionally
liberal donation. Now Donald was a Scot
who appreciated hard cash; for though he
might probably die a pensioner of Glenconan,
he meant to leave as little as possible to
chance, and hoped to guarantee himself against
old age and the rheumatism.

At the same time, he had a heart and a

conscience; and the young kinsmen of his master were charges of his own. He shook his head as he weighed the glittering coins in his palm, and then he tendered three or four of them back again.

"No, no, Mr Venables. I know, as the minister well remarked the other Sabbath, when he was giving us a discourse for the maintaining of foreign missions, that the liberal soul will be made fat—not that putting on fat is any good thing to a gentleman who cares greatly about the shooting and the stalking. But if you would forgive my saying it, when ye offered me all that gold, it brought to my mind another saying, though I am not just sure that ye will find it in the Scriptures."

"I believe I can guess, Donald," rejoined Jack, quick as a gun-flash, with a laugh and a blush. "Fools and their money—hey?— was that about it, Mr Donald?"

"It's not for the like of me to contradict your honour," said Donald, demurely. "Though, mind you, Mr Venables, I would sooner have bitten out my tongue than spoken it. But you're but a young man, sir, and I'm an old one that likes you; and—Glenconan himself, for all his open hand, would never have given half as much."

Jack, though slightly offended, stood embarrassed and self-condemned. "The old keeper is a gentleman, and I'm a snob. Well, well, Donald," he went on, "I daresay you may be right. Keep the sovereigns you did keep, and leave the rest with the minister for those missions you were speaking of. Do what you will with them, in short. At any rate, you won't refuse me a shake of the hand;" and suiting the action to the word, he grasped the hand of the keeper. Then turning on his heel, he sought Glenconan in his "study."

The "study" was of course the most uncomfortable den in the house; and the surroundings, in the shape of rods and landing-nets, account-books, &c., seemed singularly unfavourable to literary pursuits—which was of the less consequence, that the occupier was essentially a man of action, and very little of a bookworm. He listened to his nephew's piece of news with extreme satisfaction. He sympathised with the unexpressed feelings of

the young man, in that Jack was relieved from
the anxiety of laying himself under pecuniary
obligations. Like Jack, perhaps he saw omens
of good-luck in the windfall that had come in
so very opportunely. And after a short and
business - like talk, the couple came to an
identical conclusion.

"There, there! that's agreed," said Moray.
"You understand that you may count on me
to forward your views in any reasonable direction; and in the meantime, you go to Sussex
and discuss matters with your father. You
are bound to consult him before deciding on
anything."

"I could not have a more affectionate adviser, at all events," rejoined the young man,
warmly. "And with you to consult upon
practical points, I would not take a quarter
of a million for my chances. Indeed, if Mr
Philpotts had left me a quarter of a million
instead of this legacy of £10,000, all the salt
and fun would have been taken out of the
future."

All things considered, it might well have
been supposed that Jack's immediate plans
were pretty well settled, as, until he had

talked them over with his father, he was
pledged to take no decided steps. But being
a far-sighted youth, with a craving for sympathy, he thought that it might be well to
take his cousin into his confidence. As she
might probably be profoundly interested in
that future of his, it was only fair that he
should have her views about it.

And a less impressionable heart than Jack's
might have been touched by the unfeigned
delight with which she heard of his good fortune. Indeed natural vanity was nearly per-
suading him that she must feel a personal
interest in the matter.

" What a dear, thoughtful old gentleman
Mr Philpotts must have been ! What a pity
he lived and died a bachelor ? " she added,
sympathetically.

" I don't know about that," laughed Jack.
" You see, if he had left half-a-dozen of chil
dren, I should certainly have never come in for
my legacy. And," he went on, more seriously,
" it may be a matter of the last importance to
me."

For Jack was already half forgetting himself in indulging his new sense of freedom.

Penniless, he had undertaken to do nothing in the way of love-making ; but now he felt that he was hardly breaking faith in feeling his way for his own satisfaction.

Grace evidently did not understand him in any way. She raised her arched eyebrows with a certain subdued scorn, and her delicate nostril curled with something like contempt. Having always had the command of money, she thought very little of it ; and though a handsome legacy might doubtless be a subject for congratulation, anything like excessive appreciation of it struck her as sordid.

Jack saw the unfortunate impression he had made, and regretted a false step. If he did not explain and apologise, he might do himself irreparable injury with the woman with whom he most desired to stand well. On the other hand, he remembered the promise to her father. His usual presence of mind forsook him, and he stammered, hesitated, and turned painfully red. His confusion served him better than the plainest speech. Grace, with ready feminine intuition, more than half suspected the truth. She rapidly followed Jack's mental struggles, and coloured up like him as she reproached herself for having misconceived him. She fancied she understood the delicacy that had dictated his reserve ; she knew that she had nothing to fear in the shape of a precipitate proposal : the blush died away as she recovered self-command, and her composure contrasted with her cousin's confusion. Confused as he was, Jack was quick-sighted as usual. He had seen the blush, and it considerably cheered him, though he did not attach undue importance to it.

"What a deal of luck there is in this world!" he reflected. "If my face had not played me false for once, I must have gone away leaving Grace in utter ignorance ; and then, who knows what might have happened? She might have come to like Leslie as well as I do—or better."

Then, with something of the wisdom of the serpent, he made an excuse to bring the interview to a conclusion, and left his pretty cousin to her meditations. But being a right-minded youth in the main, and honourable to boot, the idea that he had betrayed himself troubled his conscience. "If my uncle knew what has passed, he might have good reason to be indignant. It was no fault of mine, to be sure ; but appearances would be decidedly against me. I believe that the straightest course is the safest, and that I ought to go to him and make a clean breast of it."

And as he feared to go back on that bold resolution, he struck while the iron was hot, and went straight to his uncle. Do what he would, or blunder as he might, it seemed that his conduct was to commend him to that gentleman. Moray shook his head as he listened to the confession, but at the same time admired his nephew's candour.

"Well, as you say, perhaps you were hardly to blame ; and as yet, at least, there can be no great harm done. Grace's heart is free, and you are going to leave us to-morrow." At which double-barrelled delivery of small-shot Jack winced perceptibly. And he flinched still more unmistakably when this eccentric father went on—

"You have been frank enough with me— too frank, perhaps, with Grace ; and so, for her sake, and to countercheck that uncontrollable move of yours, I am decided to be as frank with Leslie as with you, and more frank

than I had intended. You agree with me—
and it strikes me that Leslie is of our opinion
—that Grace is a girl in a thousand. Hitherto
she has seen next to nothing of society. She
will marry, of course, sooner or later; but
there is no need to press her upon any man."
Jack half interrupted with a gesture of indignant protest, but Moray went on imperturba-
bly. "There is no need, I say, to throw her
at any man; and, as I told you before, I shall
not attempt to influence her choice, so long as
she sets her affections on a gentleman of birth,
with a spotless character and decent means.
I mentioned, too, that she may not be so rich
as you suppose. Be that as it may, she must
not be hurried to commit herself, by her feelings, or her fancy, or anything else. I don't
know much about young ladies or their fancies, more's the pity; but it strikes me that
this secret of yours which she has surprised,
may fill her thoughts to her harm, and she
may possibly build up a romance on it before
we know where we are. I promised you fair-
play, but nothing more; and my daughter is
nearer and dearer to me than you can be, so I
shall speak to Leslie as I have spoken to you,

and leave him to regulate his conduct accordingly. From the first, Grace shall have the chance of selection, so far as her limited opportunities go. Moreover, when Leslie has left us, and before the beginning of the grouse-shooting, I shall carry her off, by way of distraction, to pay some visits. There are old family friendships that ought to be renewed, and it is high time she saw something more of her fellow-creatures."

And Moray's keen grey eyes, that nevertheless had much of the kindness of his daughter's, looked straight into those of his young favourite. Original or eccentric as his conduct might be, Mr Venables was persuaded that he knew his own mind, and was acting on some principle, however peculiar—and to a certain extent he did understand, being anything but dull of perception. So far, in all honour and good-nature, they were exchanging passes with the foils. Jack had been more than indiscreet in giving Grace a glimpse at the state of his feelings. Moray parried and returned the thrust by putting Leslie forward as a probable rival, besides opening up a vista of possibilities in the shape of eligible young

men in pleasant country-houses. Mr Venables
was to have fair-play, but no particular favour;
and in the reaction from sanguine expectation
to sad despondency, he felt that, in spite of
his legacy and his hopes, he was still a mere
outsider in the betting. So that Moray's
quickly delivered thrust had touched just as
he might have intended. At the same time,
mortified and disappointed as he was, Jack
could not help exercising his active mind on
the metaphysical problem presented to it.

" I've heard and seen something of match-
making mothers, but hang me if I understand
this match-making father! He's devoted to
his daughter, as well he may be; he starts
from the incontrovertible truth that he need
not throw her at anybody's head; he's a man
of the world, if ever there was one,—and yet
he practically offers Grace to me or to Leslie,
and apparently proposes, moreover, to hawk her
about in half the houses of the Highlands, as
if he were bound to match her against time
under heavy penalties. What I see most
clearly in the business is, that he credits Leslie
and me with the tempers of angels, or he
would never cast such an apple of discord

between us. But if I do have Ralph for a rival, it shall be all fair and above - board between us. I don't forget that I owe him my life, though the time may come when it will cost me something to remember it."

And indeed Moray, who meant excellently well by both his young kinsmen, being chiefly preoccupied with the future of his child, had altogether ignored the awkward complications that might come of the stirring up of angry passions. Undoubtedly the fond father, unconsciously to himself, seemed to be playing the mischief - maker as well as the matchmaker.

CHAPTER VIII.

A MEETING AT THE CROSS-TRACKS.

WHEN Jack Venables spoke of standing in
hesitation at cross-ways on the road of life, he
did not carry the metaphor quite so far as he
might have done. Were we favoured by the
sight of a sketch-map of our track through the
world, we should see that there were side-paths
perpetually branching off, which to all appear-
ance we might just as probably have followed
to our misfortune or our signal advantage.
While in any general biographical chart, illus-
trating the career of sundry individuals, we
should see the paths of others striking into our
own by the most unexpected turns at the least
likely places ; so that two men thrown together
by accident or Providence shall thereafter walk
on together side by side, or possibly even arm
in arm.

As he fancied, it was nothing more than a
caprice which decided Mr Venables to go south
by sea, instead of establishing communications
with the Southern Express at Perth. As he
remarked to his uncle, whom he still politically
took into his confidence, " I may as well think
matters quietly over, before having a serious
talk with my father: it will be better that I
have something cut and dry to suggest."

Moray, of course, made no objection: the
route by which his young friend might travel
was a matter of perfect indifference to him.
As for Jack, he knew himself too well to
imagine that he could ever think when he
wished to think. With his mercurial disposition and nervous temperament, he put far more
faith in quick inspirations, influenced by consideration of circumstances on the spur of the
moment, or possibly by the chapter of accidents. But he had resolved to embark on one
of the Highland coasting - steamers at Port
Sligachan, simply because he liked the idea
of a sea-voyage.

The very day he settled that impromptu
plan, a gentleman of sympathetic nature,
though, as the Americans say, an entire

stranger to him, came to a similar decision in the Isle of Skye. The Honourable Wilfred Winstanley had all his life been addicted to impulses, though he nevertheless had made his way in the world very successfully. One night he had gone to bed in the state-chamber of Castle Somerled in a less serene frame of mind than was usual with him. For the most part he was good-nature itself, as a man ought to be on whom fortune had smiled very steadily. His host's Lafitte had tasted sour; there had been no savour in the *entrées;* he had been vexed to find himself "doggish and snappish," as a worthy Quaker used to remark in his diary. Altogether, when he took his bedroom candle to go up-stairs he felt strangely out of sorts, and he went to bed to toss and tumble under the blankets. Towards the small hours his sensations gave shape to his suspicions, and he turned out of bed into the dawn to confirm these.

"Gout, by Jove! I thought as much," was his rueful verdict, as he gazed on a swelling toe that blushed under his anxious examination. "Gout, by Jove! and I'll be bound Willis has brought no colchicum. It's true that I have

not had an attack for a couple of years. Just
like my luck," he added, with the fractious in-
justice of a spoiled child; "it's choosing to lay
hold of me in this heaven-forsaken Patmos,
where the doctors are sure to smell of spirits
and peat-smoke, and their drugs can't be worth
the bottles they put them in. Well, if I am to
be ill, I'll be ill in Berkeley Square,—always
supposing I don't break down in making a bolt
for it."

And when Willis appeared with his master's
hot water, he received orders to make inquiries as to steamers, but to pack immediately in any case.

"Should no steamer be expected to-day,
you will go and bargain for a tug, or something of that kind."

And Willis, who had been broken to passive
obedience, and who had long before ceased to
be surprised at anything, if he shrugged his
shoulders metaphorically, simply answered
with a "Yes, sir."

As it happened, a cargo-steamer, carrying
passengers when it could pick them up, had
come the day before into the adjacent harbour, and having received prompt despatch

from the company's agents, was prepared to weigh anchor in the forenoon. Lord Somerled, Mr Winstanley's noble host, protested vehemently against his friend's departure. Mr Winstanley was profuse of apologies, but inflexible. It was altogether for Lord Somerled's sake that he left. He had made a rule of never being laid up in a friend's house when he could help it, and it was a rule he had never hitherto departed from.

"Nothing would tempt me to victimise you, my dear fellow. It would be flying in the face of all my principles. I hope I'm unselfish before everything, and I know my duty to my neighbour better than that."

So his lordship did what the valet did not venture on. He presumed on a long acquaintance so far as to shrug his shoulders openly, and ordered the carriage to drive Mr Winstanley to the harbour.

To do Mr Winstanley bare justice, however precipitate his impulses, he acted upon them with rare determination. Even to himself he would have been loath to acknowledge that, "not to put too fine a point on it," he had made a fool of himself. Yet we will not

undertake to say that he had not some search-
ings of heart, when he hobbled on his sounder
fòot across the greasy decks of the Cuchullin.
We could almost aver that when he was as-
sisted down the battered brass-bound steps of
the dark companion, and had stumbled into
the gloom of his strong-smelling little cabin,
he wafted a sigh of soft regret towards the
comfortable quarters he had precipitately
quitted. If he suffered, however, like the
impenitent cardinal, he "made no sign"; and
suffer he certainly did, in body if not in spirit.
The shaking of a carriage is far from being a
sovereign specific for a sharp attack of gout
that has quickly developed itself. If we were
to give a non - professional diagnosis of his
symptoms, we should say that he felt as if
the roomy slipper he was wearing had suddenly become several sizes too small for him ;
as if a cook had been scientifically scoring the
ailing foot in the fashion in which you prepare
a spatch-cocked chicken, subsequently rubbing
in the mustard and Worcester sauce, not by
any means forgetting the cayenne ; and as if
a spark or two from the glowing kitchen-fire
had flown and lodged themselves under the

toe - nail.   In such circumstances the Stoic
may make no sign, but his temper will not
be of the sweetest.

When his blinking eyes had accustomed
themselves to the dimness, Winstanley cast a
disconsolate glance around him.   The low-
roofed cabin showed wear and tear, and the
panels stood sorely in need of repainting.
The table and the seats in the centre were
fixtures, and it needed dexterous navigation
to thread the narrow passage between them
and the surrounding lockers and horse-hair
sofas ; while a man over the middle height,
unless he stooped his head, must infallibly
bump it against the blackened beams above.
But, Mr Winstanley, though he loved his lux-
uries, was an old traveller : he had been in
queer places and seen strange things ; nor did
he expect in a Hebridean cattle-boat to find
the comforts of a Cunard Liner.   Had it not
been for that abominable gout, he would have
enjoyed the novel experience rather than
otherwise.   And, the gout notwithstanding,
he merely made a grimace when the shock-
headed and courteous individual who offici-
ated as steward, in answer to his inquiry as

to an available berth, pointed to one of the tattered sofas.

"Ye see, sir, we're no just that weel provided with state-cabins," said the man apologetically, as if some half-dozen were already engaged, and they would have arranged to have one or two more had they expected his honour's arrival.

"If only I have no companions in my misery," murmured Winstanley, resignedly; and supporting himself on his valet's shoulder, he painfully regained the deck. But even that very natural wish was not to be gratified.

"I guess, stranger, I must have done you a mischief, and seems, judging from your limp when you came aboard, that you had been sorter crippled already."

The apology, such as it was, came from a lank, wiry figure, in a tall stove-pipe hat, and a suit of go-to-meeting garments; and Winstanley, although he had been repeatedly in America, detested Americans of a certain class. And assuredly an apology of some sort was due, since this particular citizen of the States had brought down his foot upon Mr Winstanley's afflicted member, making that dignified

gentleman *pirouette* on one leg, with his hand
on his servant's shoulder as the pivot of the
movement.   Hobbling off in rage and pain,
he did not care to prolong the conversation ;
but the ejaculation he uttered, when beyond
ear-shot of his assailant, made a Scotch minister, similarly attired in black, turn up his eyes
in silent protestation.   It was seldom that
Mr Winstanley so far forgot himself.   He
hated the clergyman for that silent reproof,
but he was still more annoyed with himself
for having given cause for it.

Ere he had forgiven himself or regained his
composure, the vessel was under way.   She
was a narrow, deep-waisted screw, indifferently
manned, and apparently much overloaded.
At least it struck our friend, who had been at
sea in all manner of craft, that she was down
by the head and thoroughly out of trim.   She
carried a load of sheep and black cattle forward, besides a score or two of Celts, who
might be bound for the herring-fishing ; and
the deck abaft the funnel was hampered with
a miscellaneous pile of mixed goods, so that
her few hands had little room to move about.
" I hope we may have fair weather," was his

passing prayer; but his mind was chiefly preoccupied with his malady, as was only natural.
The stamp of the American's heavy boot was
still throbbing and thrilling through all his
fevered pulses; and as the green shores of the
land-locked bay seemed to slip past the sta
tionary steamer, he paid no sort of attention
to the scenery. But as a sense of soothing
succeeded to acute torments, a change came
over the spirit of his dreams. The American's
violent remedy had brought temporary relief:
instead of being worse, he felt decidedly better. And in that he saw a direct interposition
of the Providence which had consistently befriended him through his many wanderings.
He had prided himself on always making the
best of mankind as he found them, and here
was an opportunity of rising to the occasion—
of coming out strong, like Mr Tapley under
adverse circumstances. He would make the
best of the circumstances, unpromising as
they were, and show himself more than civil
to the uncongenial companions of his solitude.
An almost miraculous lull in his pains con-
firmed him in his manly resolutions. And
when the tinkling of a cracked bell announced

the serving of an early dinner, he almost felt
equal to the occasion.   In fact, having merely
broken his fast upon tea and toast, and being
a man of active habits, and by no means,
generally speaking, a gouty subject, the crav-
ings of nature began to assert themselves.

He was pleased to find the cabin comparatively well ventilated.   The active Mr Willis
had persuaded the steward to open one or two
of the bull's-eyes and admit a current of air.
Four gentlemen had already taken their
places at a table seated for a dozen : there
was his American acquaintance opposite to
the minister ; while the skipper, who occupied
the place of honour at the top, was faced by a
sheep-farmer from " misty Skye," bound on a
pleasure-jaunt to the western metropolis of
Scotland.

There is no nobler sight for gods or men
than " a great man struggling with the storms
of fate."   Cato-like, the Honourable Mr Winstanley had screwed himself up to a pitch
of philosophy, where he was not to be lightly
shaken.   He scarcely flinched, so far as could
be seen in the dusky twilight of the cabin,
when the American welcomed him with the

cordiality of an old acquaintance, whose friendly offices had given a claim on his goodwill.

"Wal, stranger," exclaimed that really good fellow, with a warmth that meant a hearty introduction to the company,—"wal, stranger, here you are, all slicked up and smoothed down. Guess, when you limped aft with the broken balance of you, after I had most crushed off that gouty foot of yourn, the bristles were up along the back like a cata-mount. That was human natur', and I apolo-gise. You remembered me of old Jeb Peabody and Judge Mason's bull. You want to hear about it, you say. Wal, Jeb was ferryman at Salem Flats on the Chickabody river, and he kept a liquor-bar, and a store for general rations to the back of that. All-fired deaf he was, ever since he had been hoisted by mis-take, when the boys forgot him, over a blastin' charge in a quartz-mine down to Denver. He could take a power of drink could Jeb, but he was apt to get drowsy over it in a general way. Wal, one night he was sitting nodding behind his pipe in his shanty, when he hears somebody a-tapping at the door. 'Come in,' says Jeb, still sleepy-like. The party on the wrong side of the shingles raps again. 'Come in,' says Jeb again, 'or else, I guess, though it's well on in the fall, you'll find it kinder warm when you do come.' The stranger outside seemed deaf like Jeb; 'peared he was gettin' riled with being kept a-waitin', for soon Jeb could hear him stampin' and cussin'. 'Wal,' remarks Jeb, with a sigh, 'if I must get up to open, I must; but I guess, my friend, I'll make you see stars—some,' and he reaches out his hand to his slip of hickory,—when all of a suddint the shingles cave in, and Judge Mason's bull is in Jeb Peabody's weskit. Jeb was a candid man, and as he said arterwards in mentioning the fact—'the way I shouted and slipped out o' the winder like a greased streak o' lightnin', afore the crittur was done prancin' around, was a caution to iled snakes.' And that was you, stranger, as you hollered and made tracks; and as for me, like the judge's bull, I guess I was too fur taken aback to apologise."

No one seemed greatly to appreciate the American's apologue or apology, which, considering there was but an ounce or two of the

pure metal to some tons of quartz, was not
much to be wondered at. But Winstanley
felt more in charity towards him than before,
since he saw that the transatlantic gentleman
was well disposed to monopolise the talk, and
that for himself he might play the part of
listener. During dinner and afterwards, the
voluble American sought to beguile the time
with a fund of anecdote, of aphorism, and sage
and moral reflection. Nevertheless, he did not
have it all his own way by any means. The
minister and the sheep-farmer had many subjects more or less in common—mammon, home-
missions, markets, the clip of wool, the *outre-
cuidance* of the crofters, and the oppression of
the landowners. As for the skipper, he seldom
opened his mouth, except to stow away the
very solid victuals, or swallow whisky-and-
water. On the whole, Winstanley, not fore-
seeing what was to befall on the morrow,
deemed him the most agreeable member of
the party.

The supper, which came off at nine, was
more successful than the dinner. After de-
vouring everything indigestible, from cold
corned-beef to crabs and Welsh rabbit, the

society settled down to steady drinking. The American, to do him justice, having taken a "cocktail or two" by way of digestive, stuck thenceforward to aerated water. But he talked nine to the dozen, as he chewed plugs of golden Virginia indefatigably, in deference to the scruples of his new English friend, who had strongly protested against smoking. Not that Mr Winstanley disliked a cigar, but he objected to suffocation by rancid nicotine.

The minister, the sheep-farmer, and the skipper met on common ground, or rather on common spirits-and-water, over a bowl of punch that was brewed by the reverend gentleman, after the soundest traditions of the fathers of the Church.

"The stuff you brew at the preachings," observed the hillman, with a solemn wink, "or when you're seeking to come over the heritors for an augmentation, or an 'eke' to the manse." And worthy Dr M'Tavish, knowing well what his friend meant, fully met his expectations. Winstanley, who sat sipping some weak brandy-and-water, soon sought a refuge on the deck. But a mist that was very much of a drizzle was settling down thickly, and Willis

was almost immediately at his elbow, like a
warning conscience. For Willis was attached
to his master, and detested the duty of acting
as sick-nurse to an aggravating patient.

"Excuse me, sir, but this mist is the worst
thing in the world for you. We should say it
had set in for settled wet in the south. Believe
me, you had much better go below."

"But I am half-suffocated already, Willis,
and those good gentlemen seem to have no
notion of going to bed."

"Better be half smothered or half stunned,
sir, than suffer pain for weeks to come," answered Willis, sententiously. "The one will
be soon over ; but who can tell the end of the
other ?"

So his master yielded to reason, and de-
scended again to the Inferno, where his worst
anticipations were fully realised. If the prac-
tice of patience be the discipline of life, Winstanley should have passed a profitable night.

When he crept on to the deck in the
morning, he felt a doubly injured man. In
his sense of intense feverishness it seemed
as if he were suffering vicariously for the
indulgences of his shipmates — as if he had

swallowed the contents of the punch-bowls, while they had been simply looking on. But he revived in the freshness of the morning air, as he feasted his eyes on a magnificent Highland panorama. The Cuchullin was lying at anchor in the land-locked roadstead of Loch Rona. A thick undergrowth of dwarf oaks and alders, interlacing their bows in great beds of bracken, came literally down to the beach of shingle; half-a-dozen streams were descending so many picturesque glens, breaking here and there over tiny waterfalls; while huge hills, with slopes of the softest green, and great shoulders draped in purple heather, were backed up by the splintered and weather-worn peaks that were partially veiled in the swirl of a drifting cloudland. In the foreground, near a little "change-house" (*Anglicè*, public-house) and a cluster of hovels, was a snug shooting-box, with its garden washed by the sea-waves, where the luxuriance of the shrubs and the flower-beds glorified the warmth of the Gulf-stream.

"The boat will be going ashore, sir, after breakfast, should you think well of that," said the shock-headed steward very civilly; and

Winstanley thanked him as civilly and declined, although, to a man in his situation, the proposal sounded seductively. He would have liked nothing better than a temporary escape from his floating purgatory; but he was reconciled to his fate in remaining on board, when the sprightly American came up with his greeting.

"I 'calculate, Colonel, by the way you're sniffing the mountain air, you feel as fresh this morning as a four-year-old mustang. And if you're good for a run ashore, I'll come along and kinder take care o' you. No? You won't? Wal, then, if you like a hobble better, you're welcome to try one. Them rocks up there may be almighty grand, but I'd sooner spekilate on their tallness any day than climb them."

The morning passed slowly enough while the Cuchullin was leisurely landing cargo. The captain smoked and sipped his whisky-and-water, leaving the superintendence of operations to his mate. Winstanley, after sundry unsuccessful attempts to kill time, gave himself over to reflections that were exceedingly unpleasant. He was condemned to two other days and nights of confinement in his present society before being landed at a Christian port in the Clyde. He made up his mind to the inevitable, in the spirit of an early martyr.

And the inevitable promised to be worse than he imagined. As the day went on, in the bay, sheltered on three sides, scarcely a breath of air was stirring. But nevertheless a growing ground - swell came rolling round the bold headland to the westward. The sky had clouded over; there was oppression in the air; the leaden - coloured rollers seemed sullenly smoothed down by oil; and the mate made the remark that the glass was tumbling.

" There has been wild weather in the At-lantic—there can be no doubt of that; and the question is, whether we will not have a storm on the coast here."

As for the captain, casting all his cares upon Providence, he smoked and drank on imper-turbably.

The passengers had come on board: the Cuchullin had got up her steam, and was slew-ing her head round to the sea-channel, when

the mate sang out to slacken speed. A boat
was seen putting out from the shore, and a
signal-flag was being waved in front of the
public-house.

"Now who may that be?" muttered Winstanley to himself. "It never rains but it
pours, and here comes another ruffian to prove
the possible aggravation of the least tolerable
calamities."

For a man was seated in the stern-sheets as
the boatmen strained to the oars.

Winstanley prided himself on his quick
perceptions, and it struck him at once that
the new-comer was a gentleman. Then the
stranger's luggage was presumptive evidence
in that direction, since it consisted of a couple
of neat portmanteaus, a gun-case, and a handbag in Russian leather. The handbag bore
the golden initial letters "J. V."; and the
gun-case, as the shrewd reader may have supposed, was superscribed at length as belonging
to John Venables, Esq.

Jack was not gouty—far from it. On the
contrary, he was in the highest health and
spirits; and he swung himself up the side
ladder with the grace of a young Antinous.

His first words were a polite apology to the captain for delaying him, which the captain acknowledged by inarticulate mutterings, and a stare from his whisky-sodden eyes.

As for Winstanley, he was from the first attracted to the stranger. Here, according to outward appearances, was a man with whom he might possibly have common ideas and sympathies. So the pair made friends over the dinner - table, and, had it not been for the interruptions of the irrepressible Yankee, would practically have monopolised the conversation. For the minister was overawed by consciousness of ignorance of the subjects the others discussed in a kind of easy freemasonry; and the sheep-farmer, like naturally modest men, was always in extremes, and either painfully shy or brilliantly audacious.

It was just as well for Mr Winstanley that he had found a companion he fancied, for it seemed likely that the voyage might be indefinitely prolonged. The night had settled down in a fog, denser and damper than that of the previous one; and ten hours after they started the steamer was going half-speed over a heavy ground-swell in impenetrable darkness. Slowing the engines had been the result of a compromise, when the skipper in a moment of drunken depression had lent an ear to the warnings of his inexperienced mate. But when the youth, in increasing uneasiness, urged lying off altogether till day should dawn, his superior had lost temper and decided to go boldly ahead.

"It's but kittle steering here," the mate had objected; "and with all that corrugated iron in the hold we can hardly trust altogether to the compasses. If we were among the rocks and reefs off the Point of Achnahullichan now——"

"And what if we were, my man?" returned his commander, with drunken dignity. "Man and boy, I've been afloat for thirty years, and I ought to know every one of the reefs between Cape Wrath and the Moil of Cantyre."

They were bending over a chart spread on the cabin-table, and the little company of passengers was grouped around them.

"There's one of the reefs, then, I calculate," ejaculated the American, dryly, and with infinite promptitude.

For as the captain spoke there was a shock
and a long shivering, a rending of timber, and
a tremulous rasping that had run along the
ship's keel like electricity, communicating with
the passengers through their shaking limbs,
and shooting a thrill to each nerve and fibre;
while simultaneously rose shrill cries and wild
shouts from the decks.   Then came another
shock, like the despairing struggle of a stranded
whale, and a duller sound of the splintering of
timbers.

CHAPTER IX.

THE SHIPWRECK.

WINSTANLEY forgot his gout as the captain was suddenly sobered. There was a rush for the deck in that first alarm, as of men who preferred to perish in the open, rather than to be drowned below decks like rats and cockroaches. Once on the deck there was little to be seen, but a great deal to be heard. The lantern gave but a fitful light, throwing faint reflections on the grey wreaths of watery vapour. But out of the darkness, that was to be felt rather than seen, came appalling evidences of a general panic. The Highland forecastle passengers, more accustomed to their hills than to the sea, had lost their heads, and were bellowing and "routing" like the cattle. And the cattle, where they had not broken from the fastenings, had been jumbled together

in prostrate heaps, and were plunging madly
in the efforts to regain their legs. The more
placidly minded sheep were bleating piteously;
the ship was groaning, though it could not
roll, in response to the surf that was dashing
against its sides; and the funnel was belching
forth volumes of steam and flaming showers of
sparks, for something had gone wrong with
the fires or the machinery.

In the darkness and the turmoil, so far as
could be judged, there were only four men
who had kept their heads. These were the
young mate, the shock-headed steward, the
cool American, and Mr Jack Venables. As
for Mr Winstanley, he was in mortal alarm,
though he had too much self-respect to show
it; and, rather to give himself time to calm
down than for any better reason, he addressed
a remark to Mr Venables, who happened to be
close by his side, and was busy stripping off
coat and boots.

" It's all over with us, I suppose."

But Jack's courage was of the kind that is
highest in emergencies, and his spirits rose
buoyantly to the excitement of danger.

" Not if I know it, sir. We may all get

away in the boats ; and if not, I mean to try to save myself by swimming. The steamer is upon rocks, and one may find a footing on them, till some passing vessel comes to take us off."

Thus having spoken on the spur of the moment, the selfishness of his speech struck him. "I wish this crippled old gentleman had not been here,"—so, we may suppose, ran the current of his thoughts. "But as he is here, I am bound to see him through it, worse luck." And then he added, " If you keep by me, or rather, stay by the companion here, I shall come back before I leave, and will gladly give you a helping hand."

Hardly even when talking to Mr Moray, had Jack ever invested words to better purpose. And indeed in this case, Winstanley had reason to be doubly grateful. Not only did the calmness of the young stranger help him to regain his self-possession, but it was a promise of self-sacrifice which he felt assured would be redeemed. So whether his feelings were too much for him or not, he merely squeezed the young gentleman's hand by way of answer.

While we have been lingering over this conversation apart between the only two people in whom we are greatly interested, incidents were being fast crowded into seconds. Had it been daylight, one might have looked on at a veritable panic. The Celts in the steerage had sufficiently recovered from their stupor to be seriously alarmed. They had animal courage enough, but it was ill adapted to unfamiliar circumstances. They made a rush at the boats, and carried them by storm. Their frenzied impetuosity knocked a hole in the bottom of one, which happened to be loaded with coils of wire fencing. As for the other, by the aid of the seamen it was lowered into the water *tant bien que mal*. But that boat was to the windward side of the ship, and the surf was strong, and the gear slightly fouled at one end. Naturally the boat upset under a cascade of human beings, most of them weighing considerably over fourteen stone ; and then it became a case of "save who can," for no one had a thought to bestow upon his neighbours. Two or three who fell struggling in the deeper water, were swept to sea or under the ship's counter, and were seen no more.

The rest, to their surprise and pleasure, regained their legs, and were either washed up
against the swamped boat and the swinging
tackle, or, clutching wildly at each other,
their feet struck on the rocks, up which they
scrambled through the shoaling water, till,
clinging to the slippery sea-weed like limpets,
they had time for recollection and a long
breath.   Then one or two, with more presence
of mind than the others, shouted out that
there was firm footing under the ship's bows ;
and when the good news had slowly circulated
on board, relief from the apprehension of immediate danger brought about a wonderful reaction.   Their safety need only be a question
of time, and the indolent side of the excitable
Highlanders turned upwards again.

And with a falling ground-swell and calm
weather they might have been well contented
to wait indefinitely.   But as the first breaking
of the dawn began to streak the eastern sky,
there came an ominous sighing and whistling
through the shrouds and the funnel-stays,
which caused the mate and the shock-headed
steward to prick their ears and exchange
significant glances.   The wind was getting

up, as the glass had prognosticated a gale ; and when the waves rose with the wind, the Cuchullin would probably go to pieces. Nor, as the breaking of the day made objects visible, was the sight of the reef on which they were hard and fast by any means reassuring. Low and rugged, and covered with slimy brown and green sea-weed, it looked very like the slippery back of the fabulous kraken, and nearly as likely to be submerged at any moment. Assuredly it was sunk far out of sight in spring-tides ; probably the seas washed over it in such a gale as was coming on.

The captain, although comparatively sobered by the catastrophe, was dazed, and disposed to take gloomy views, as he well might be, considering that under the most favourable circumstances his certificate was sure to be suspended by the Board of Trade. So he declared that as the vessel might break up at any moment, the passengers had better take refuge on the reef, which might be trusted not to go to pieces, though it was quite on the cards that it might be swamped.

Had an unimaginative artist sought materials for the illustration of ' Robinson Crusoe,'

assuredly he might have found them in the
scene on the reef, which was locally known as
the " Kittiwake's neb." The steerage passengers began by saving their personal property,
and piled bags and blankets and wooden
" kists " about them. Then, for sheer want
of occupation, and by the offer of free rations
of " Tallisker," they were persuaded by the
mate and the steward to unload the live cargo.
We can't say that humanity had much to do
with it. So half - wild cattle that had the
strength and suppleness of the famous Chil-
lingham herd, were persuaded to leap from the
deck into the water. The sheep followed their
leaders, when one or two had been caught up
and pitched over bodily. And then there was
a scene, such as might have been witnessed
when the ark brought up, after its seven
months' cruise, on Mount Ararat. The cattle
crowded together, as is their custom, with
stooping heads and staring coats, playfully
goring each other in the ribs with their tremendous horns, till the melancholy ocean re-
sounded with their bellowing. The sheep, that
jostled up against the oxen, although confining
themselves to plaintive protests against their

bad luck, were scarcely in the sum total less
vociferous. We daresay the rats left the
stranded ship, though, had they foreseen the
fate that must befall them, they would have
stuck by her so long as she floated. But the
old cabin cat, which had slipped over the side
when his betters set him the example, was
perhaps more to be felt for than any person.
He lowered himself over the side, from a
natural instinct of self-preservation ; but really
he cared very little what became of him. He
was too miserable, as he picked his way among
pools of sea-water, and set down his feet gin-
gerly on rocks that were slimy with trailing
sea-weed. His principles and his instincts
denied him the resource of suicide—for we
believe that, among all the *memorabilia* of
remarkable cats, no one instance has been
recorded of an animal that drowned itself.
But he strolled recklessly under the very
noses of collies who, in ordinary circumstances,
would have made but a couple of mouthfuls of
him. As it was, in the presence of a common
danger, they saw him pass with an indifference
as appalling as his own, to any one who had
leisure to remark the phenomenon. And so

the desponding Thomas went on, till he ran up against a gentleman seated in a chair, when the domestic instincts asserted themselves, the more decidedly for the delightful surprise. He rubbed his sides against an upturned pair of trousers; he made the wearer wince by smoothing his whiskers against a muffled foot; and then he gave a flying leap out of the damp, arching his back and purring pleasantly against a woollen waistcoat.

In fact it had been a pretty though a pathetic sight to see Mr Venables piloting Mr Winstanley to the highest point of the reef, and there depositing him on one of the two or three cane-bottomed chairs to be found on board the Cuchullin. Willis, who was still amenable to orders, though he had lost all power of initiation, followed, carrying the dressing-case that was placed under his master's feet. And there sat the Honourable Wilfred Winstanley, gathering the skirts of a trailing ulster round his legs, more painfully sensible than ever of his signal folly in flying so hastily from his comfortable quarters at Somerled. But if he had a feeling stronger than that of self-reproach, it was of gratitude

to the cheery young fellow who had done
so much for him. Already Winstanley
had asked his name, and had been duly informed. To say nothing of Jack's sanguine
spirit being contagious, it was difficult to
seem depressed when the youth was near.
He would have sat self-rebuked while Mr
Venables was quietly conversing, as if they
had come together in a club smoking-room in
Pall Mall. We will not undertake to say that
there was not some swagger about Mr Venables, but are content merely to record how
he behaved.

" I should prefer a cigarette, as I have gone
without breakfast. But 'needs must be,'—
you know the proverb, sir ; so, by your leave,
though I think I heard them say you objected
to smoking, I shall light a pipe. If I keep
well to leeward, perhaps you won't mind."

But after a few whiffs of the pipe, a fresh
idea seemed to strike him.

" What a picturesque sight it is, and what
comical groups of figures these are in the
foreground ! Gray's odes come back to the
memory. Confusion, fright, ay, and famine
too, and ever so many more realistic concep-

tions of the passions. And what a bit that is,
à la M. Gudin at the Luxembourg, for example, where the waves are breaking against
the sides of the old ship, with the sea-weed
streaming on the curl of the surf, and boxes
and trunks bobbing about among the breakers."

And from another of the numerous pockets
in his shooting-jacket he produced something
between a memorandum-book and a sketch-
book, and, smiling, proceeded to draw. Winstanley looked at him curiously. His hand
was steady and his eye was clear, and he
handled the pencil for all the world as if he
had been sitting on a camp-stool in some
sequestered glen, with an immediate prospect
of muffins and coffee. Jack marked the
glance, and answered it in about five minutes,
by carelessly passing his sketch-book to Winstanley.

"Admirable, sir, admirable!" was that
gentleman's verdict; for in fact his young
companion, by some sharp and bold touches,
had given a very fair idea of water in motion;
while the rendering of the more prominent
figures in the foreground was a clever blend-
ing of the grotesque with the veracious. And

though he immediately dismissed the matter from his mind, the memory of it afterwards did Jack good service.

Indeed more serious considerations were soon to preoccupy him. A business of the kind must be slow at best, whether to those who figure in it or to those who read about it; so we spare our readers many of the details. But with the rising tide, driven over the reef by the winds, the water at every seventh wave or so actually washed over Winstanley's boot and slipper; and although it became pretty plain that no one need be actually drowned, it seemed probable that his constitution might be shattered for life. He was so lost in a labyrinth of gloomy thoughts, that he was indifferent even to the presence of the irrepressible American, who opined that he would rather run the chances of being sky-rocketed from high-pressure "ingines" among the snags of the Mississippi, than be cast adrift on an empty stomach in that herring-pool, when a man should be turning his attention to mutton-chops and ham-and-eggs.

Nothing could be more welcome, then, than the sight of the Clansman, steaming southward on the way to Oban. She answered the signals of distress, and bore down to the assistance of the wreck. The embarkation was a matter of time, and of some little inconvenience as well; but the reef acted as a kind of breakwater against the freshening gale, and the castaways were hospitably welcomed into snug quarters, where they had an opportunity of changing their damp garments.

"I seem to have known you from your boyhood," said Winstanley very warmly to his young acquaintance. "You have stood by me in a way I shall never forget; and as you were ready to do me one inestimable service in the way of risking your life, I mean to ask you to do me another. It's the way of the world, you know, so you need not be surprised."

"Very willingly," answered Jack, with graceful readiness—not the less readily, no doubt, that he felt instinctively that the favour to be asked was to pave the way to some return for his generous devotion.

"Well, I fancy I may take it for granted that your time is at your disposal, otherwise you would hardly have shipped for a cruise in that miserable old tub. I mean to land at

Oban, where I fear I may have to lay up and take medical advice. If you could bestow a day or two on a fretful invalid, I should feel, if possible, more grateful than I do at present." And he threw as much significance into his words as was compatible with consideration for a gentleman's feelings.

And as we know something of Mr Venables's views and nature—and as he made it a golden rule never to miss a chance—we need hardly add that he jumped at the invitation with a cordiality which greatly flattered his senior.

CHAPTER X.

A HIGHLAND TRAGEDY.

A MAN must be a bore, or a social wet blanket, if he be not missed from the society of a Highland hall. Venables was missed by his uncle; he was missed by his cousin Grace; he was missed and mourned by Donald Ross and the gillies. And, no doubt, he might have been more missed than he was by Leslie, had it not been for certain significant intimations, dropped in the course of the conversation which Glenconan had with his elder nephew according to arrangement. It is true that Mr Moray said very little, being almost inclined to repent his frankness with Jack Venables; and as he had already nearly burned his fingers, he was apprehensive of further indiscretions. Yet he did give the young laird of Roodholm to understand that Grace might

possibly take it into her head to marry, and
that for himself he had every confidence that
his daughter would choose wisely. He hinted,
moreover, that he had said much the same
thing to Venables, which was quite enough to
send Leslie to a scrutiny of his own feelings.
And now that the scrutiny was forced upon
the young man, he was surprised at the dul-
ness of his own perceptions. But once entered
on so fascinating a course of study, he made
astonishing progress; and self-communings,
illustrated by more assiduous perusals of his
cousin's pretty face, taught him a thousand
things he had scarcely suspected. Strong and
sluggish natures like his sometimes, nevertheless, answer promptly to the spur; and when
a spark is set to a slumbering passion, it burns
like the subterraneous volcanic fires in Java
or Japan, where the peaceful landscapes smile
over the fragile crust that may explode at
any moment in a violent conflagration.

As for Grace, she had rather felt towards
Leslie as her father felt. He was a man she
would have turned to in any trouble. She
believed in his honour as she did in his Chris-
tianity. She was sometimes almost startled

by the eloquent expression he gave to those
deeper emotions that were silently at work
within her. She felt that the active sympathy
of one so stanch and so earnest might be
everything in certain circumstances. Nevertheless, like her father, she rather admired
than loved him, cousins as they were, and
thrown continually into the most familiar
intercourse. But hitherto she had seen life
almost entirely on its sunny side, and so she
found herself more at home in the society of
the more voluble Mr Venables.

And hitherto, and so far, the stars in their
courses had been unquestionably fighting for
Jack. But now, as it chanced, Mr Leslie was
to have his innings at a moment when it
seemed to come to him as an interposition of
Providence.

Moray appeared one morning at the break-
fast-table with care upon his brow.

" I have got a batch of bothersome business
letters to answer, and I think that nowadays I
hate business as much as I once used to enjoy
it. And this is such a beautiful day, that it
seems all the more pity to waste it. Needs
must, however, when—you know the rest—

and there is no help for it. Suppose you and Grace arrange to do something, Leslie. I shall be all the more resigned if I know you are enjoying yourselves."

Leslie brightened up. Good-hearted as he was, and fond of his uncle, he scarcely sympathised with him in his present trial. And although generally truthfulness itself, he was guilty of a *compliment de circonstance*.

"I am sure we are very sorry, sir; but you know the motto of the Russells, 'What must be, must be.' Perhaps if you can knock off your work, you may join us later in the day." Then turning to his cousin, "What do you say, Grace? Shall we take the waggonette and the chestnuts, and drive over to Tomnahurich?"

Now the lively Grace, with all her regard for him, rather shrank from a day's *tête-à-tête* with her somewhat solemn cousin. If she had told the truth, she would have confessed that he almost frightened her; and she seldom, unless when his animated conversation made her forget herself, felt altogether at ease in his company. But on this occasion, as her father had said of his correspondence, there seemed

to be no help for it, so she resigned herself
with alacrity and a charming grace.

In fact, Tomnahurich had a mystical attraction for her—all the more so, that on the only
occasion when she had visited it, she had for
once been out of tune with her favourite companion.   Jack Venables had been at her elbow
through a brilliant afternoon, and his lively
rattle had jarred upon her sensibilities, as the
blaze of the sunshine had seemed unsuitable
to the scenery.

The waggonette with the chestnut cobs came
round, and Grace stepped up on the box-seat
by the side of her cousin.   The taciturnity of
the driver surpassed her apprehensions—one
may easily have too much of peace and calm.
Leslie seemed embarrassed and lost in thought,
although he handled the reins carefully over
the somewhat break-neck roads.   He would
talk with almost feverish fluency for a minute
or two, and then relapse into long silence.   Had
Grace been more self-conscious, she might have
feared he was on the brink of a proposal,
although assuredly nothing was further from
his thoughts ; and he was one of the last men
to throw away a game by precipitation.   She

was immensely relieved when the carriage pulled up, and the groom was left in charge to await their return, the horses being picketed on a patch of turf. Now she was no longer hand-locked to a spasmodically galvanised corpse, and could break away to gather wild flowers or on any other excuse. Her pet terrier ran yelping on ahead. Leslie loaded himself with the luncheon-basket, with a rug, and his cousin's sketch-book, and strode along by her side. The scenery was picturesque enough and wild enough. What had once been a tolerable driving-track ended where the waggonette had drawn up, and was only continued by a rough footpath, winding up a steep green hill. There were solemn associations with it too, inconsistent with picnics and luncheon hampers ; for many a century before Tomnahurich had been consecrated by the Catholic Church, and it was still sacred to the feelings and the superstitions of the neighbourhood.

If we are not abroad in our Celtic philology, Tomnahurich may be translated " the hill of the fairies " ; at all events, that is the name by which the Celts call it in the Saxon. It is a little churchyard on a bold knoll or bluff, in

the midst of which might be traced the foundations of a Romish chapel. Many generations
had died and gone to dust since the sacred
edifice was abandoned for the distant kirk of
the Reformed religion. The surrounding glens
had been depopulated by emigration, and de-
scendants of the dead folks might be flourish-
ing beyond the Atlantic, owning forest farms,
or running lumbering concerns in Canada,
speculating in shares in Wall Street, or in
grain and pork in Chicago. But still the
gillies and shepherds of the neighbourhood
would bring their dead to repose on the mound
of Tomnahurich.

"Can you not fancy," observed Leslie, as
they climbed the hill—and it must be confessed
that he might have chosen a more inspiriting
subject,—"can you not fancy the melancholy
little processions that have followed the path
we are treading? It seems to me that those
who live in loneliness like this must miss the
departed who were dear to them more than we,
who are thrown into the whirl of life and may
forget now and again, if we cannot altogether
console ourselves. We bury our dead out of
our sight, and so far we are done with them;

but in these Highland solitudes, after the
funeral as before it, do what they will, the
dead must always be with them. Look at
the peasants of the Breton coast, with their
sombre fancies, which nevertheless are sad
realities to the survivors."

Grace, although sufficiently impressionable,
was taken aback, for she happened to be thinking of the cold chicken in the basket. But
tant bien que mal, she caught the ball on the
rebound, and dropped sympathetically into her
companion's gloomy train of thought.

"And can you conceive anything more sadly
depressing than a child's funeral here in the
winter? There is no putting it off, because
the few mourners have gathered together from
great distances, perhaps hazarded their lives
in the blinding snowstorm and the snowdrifts.
And the mother, broken down by watching
and grief, is toiling up the hill behind the
little coffin; and even the father's strength
has been overtasked in digging through the
frozen ground; and the light of the cottage
has been laid to rest in a spot that is the very
abomination of bleak desolation."

With such cheerful talk they beguiled the

way, till, having reached the summit of the
grassy steep, the lonely churchyard lay full in
front of them.   Whatever it might be in the
depth of winter, the spot seemed enchanting
now.   It was on the grassy crest of a rocky
headland, surrounded on three sides by a
brawling stream.   A clump or two of venerable
yews had been dwarfed and warped by expo-
sure to the weather; and beneath and around
them, and within the dilapidated wall, were
the mounds, not a few of which were almost
level with the greensward, with a sprinkling of
grey and moss-grown headstones.   The lustre
of the noonday sun was gilding the scene he
could hardly brighten; but by way of com-
pensation, the mountains to the westward were
bathed in all the glories of his golden light.
Both Leslie and his cousin involuntarily paused,
simultaneously struck by the pathos and the
splendour of the spectacle.   A still more touch-
ing surprise was awaiting them.   As Leslie
was about to move on, Grace laid a finger on
his arm.   But it hardly needed her whispered
" Hush !" to make him stoop forward and
listen with all his ears.   There was a murmur
of childish voices, which would have sounded

strangely spirit-like had it been midnight instead of brilliant noon.

Grace stole softly forward, her cousin following. Another moment, and the chicken and her hunger were altogether forgotten.

What they saw was such a scene of unaffected grief as might have inspired the pen of a Hogg or the brush of a Wilkie. There was a newly cast mound beneath the boughs of a yew, and near the brink of the precipice. And by it a comely young woman was kneeling, her chin in her hands, her elbows on the grass, and her swimming grey eyes gazing wildly into vacancy. Though their feelings were stirred in sympathy with her grief, the onlookers nevertheless were struck by the details of the picture. Setting the refining influences of a profound sorrow aside, the mourner was graceful beyond the generality of women of her station. If her complexion was freckled and her cheek-bones were somewhat high, there was beauty with great sweetness of expression in her features. The dress was of simple black, neatly fitted to the strong yet well-shaped figure; and in the rich tresses of her hair, as they hung knitted over her

neck, the auburn and the red changed to gold
in the sunbeams. That the mother had been
forgotten in the sense of her widowhood, was
shown by the boy who was clinging to her
skirts, and scared at his mother's unwonted for-
getfulness of him. And a yet younger child,
a bright little girl, was laughing and crowing,
as she plucked at the gowans.

Leslie drew back instinctively, though the
mourning widow was both blind and deaf.
And Grace had accompanied him in a sympathetic movement, though in another moment she had retraced her steps. She could
not leave the mourner without trying to comfort her, though feeling in her heart that con-
solations must be cast away. Indeed the poor
woman scarcely acknowledged the light hand
laid upon her shoulder. She cared as little for
what was passing near her as for her children;
and the touch and the presence of the stranger
were neither profanation nor intrusion: so that
Grace, with all her earnest desire to bring help,
stood silent and abashed before that speechless sorrow. She said nothing: she stooped
and kissed the children, and then she with-
drew as quietly as her cousin had withdrawn.

But if her feelings had been moved to their depths, she was full of feminine curiosity, as she vowed to herself that those feelings should find practical relief. Strange that she should have lived for weeks in those mountain solitudes, and know nothing of some cottage tragedy that must have been enacted almost under her eyes. That a tragedy there was, there could be no doubt in the world : the woman's face was eloquent with a story of sorrow which she must find an interpreter to explain.

The interpreter was there, of course, all ready to her hand. She spoke very little to Leslie, who did not say much himself; and for once his cousin understood and admired his reticence. But she flew at Donald Ross, as he said afterwards, though with all due respect, "just as if one of the terriers had been flying at the throat of a badger."

Donald, as a rule, was ready enough to talk, especially to the young mistress he adored. But on this occasion he was reserved and embarrassed, which naturally whetted her keen curiosity. And for once Miss Grace spoke peremptorily, like her father, and went very roundly to the wished-for point.

"You understand me, Donald," she exclaimed, stamping her foot on the heather, and turning her back ostentatiously on the contents of the luncheon-basket—"you understand me, and you know what I mean to say; and so you will please to tell me everything about her."

Donald raised his stalker's hat, and scratched his grey locks in profound perplexity. He looked for help towards Mr Leslie, but Mr Leslie refused to understand him, being almost as curious on the subject as Miss Grace. Then he burst out in dire perplexity—

"Deil be in me, if there is anything I would refuse to tell you, Miss Grace, but it was Glenconan himsel'—and—— "

"Oh, if you mean that my father has forbidden you," began the young lady, with a calculated sternness which nearly drove the unfortunate retainer beside himself.

"It's not precisely that, neither, Miss Grace: if it were, you might have tied me to a hart's horns before I would have told. But you know yourself that the laird may mean much when he says little; and though you may be sure that his hand is always as open as his heart, and that the widow you were speaking of has wanted for nothing, it's my belief he would wish to keep anything from you that would be troubling you."

"Well, I see how it is," responded the young lady, softening down her tones into witching seductiveness, and breaking into a smile which went straight to Donald's heart. "My father meant for the best, but chance has been too much for him. I mean to get to the bottom of this melancholy story, and may you not just as well tell it as he? He knows even better than you that I never care to be kept waiting."

Donald looked inquiringly at Leslie. Like every one else, he had an instinctive confidence in the honour and good sense of the Laird of Roodholm. Leslie simply nodded. He knew that Grace would have her will, and she might as well have it sooner than later. If he were called upon to interfere, he could always defend her with her father. And Donald, who was full of the tale he had to tell, and who rather prided himself on his gifts as a *raconteur*, broke away in full cry at the sign, like a hound after a wounded deer.

"It's three - and - thirty years past next

Martinmas since I came first into the Strath,
and I've never known a finer lad in it than
Angus M'Intyre. No day was too long for
him, and no hill too stiff; and I have known
him bring the deer home upon his shoulders,
when the pony would have broken down in
the bogs. It was seven years ago, or it may
be six, that he was married upon John Rutherford's daughter, and brought her here. Her
father was a shepherd from the South country,
and they say that he was sore against the
match—for Rutherford was as obstinate as
one of his own tups, and would always be
set against the Highlandmen; but between
Angus and the lassie, they had their way.
That Rutherford would miss her, you may
believe; and as for Angus, many a time he
has said to me that his heart was sore and
sorry for the old man. And they had the two
bonnie children you have seen with her up at
the burying-place there. I have never married myself, Miss Grace, and I never mean to,
begging your pardon; yet I will not say but
what I have sometimes wished I was Angus.

"I may have wished it one Saturday at
even, just two months agone, if I had little

thought at the time that I would never forget that night. We had been giving a look round the braes at the back of Benavourd, for we knew that Glenconan would be down in a week or two. And Angus, he would be insisting that I was to stop with him for supper, and he would be stirring the toddy, and the glass was going round, but yet the bit wife was the cheeriest thing in the cottage. And he had told me that there was a litter of foxes in the cairn on Funachan: 'deed, and the shepherd had been complaining that very day, and he said he would need to be getting out some of the terriers and seeing after them. And so I said to him, after the last glass, that we would be seeing about them; and if it was a Providence, as the minister might say, it was a Providence of the wrong kind, but that very night I found the fox-hunter from Lochloy at the kennels.

"He's an old man is Peter—as keen after the foxes as his dogs, but as stiff as Jock Rutherford; and he would by no means stay with us over the morrow, that was the Sabbath. He was bid to be on the Monday with the tacksman in Coulin; but if we thought

well of it, he would take the cairn on Funachan
on his road. So at last I said, and always will
I rue it, that he was a wilful man, and must
have his way.

"Had it not been for Peter again, I would
have turned back upon the Sunday when we
met the minister. He said but little, but he
looked the more, and many's the time that
I have minded on it since. And there was
a beast of a raven that would follow us, croak-
ing, all the way up Glendocharty; and Mary
—that's the woman ye saw, Miss Grace—she
would have keepit back Angus from going
with us, for both of them were dressed and
bound for the kirk. And Angus himself, for
once, was not that willing, but he said that if
we were set upon it, he was to show us the
place; so he whistled upon Smourach, his bit
terrier, and gave a kiss and a smile to the
wife.

"The bitch fox had gone to her earth but
little before us, and the dogs had opened on
the scent or ever we got near to the cairn.
And Peter likes ill that any should interfere
with his pack, so Angus had picked up Smourach, and was holding her in his arms. Well,

the big fox-hounds they stood whining and
scraping outside; and terrier after terrier
would be sent in among the rocks, and when
we laid our ears to the ground we could
hear the fighting and the scratching. But the
vixen, she had the best of them; and dog
after dog came back, blown and bleeding, and
the day was getting on, and Peter growing
desperate. It was then that Smourach made
a spang out of Angus's arms, though I well
believe he could have held her had it pleased
him; but he was proud of the bit thing, and
would always say that when once she put in
her teeth, the worse she was worried the
deeper they went.

"But you are wearying, and I am coming
to an end, and a doleful end it was for Angus.
The battle had begun worse than before, and
we all of us were lying and listening, when
some of the stones slippit from beneath us.
Angus was like a man distracted, for the way
was closed, and unless we could open it out
again, he had looked his last upon poor
Smourach. So he said it behoved him to
go in, and when I looked in his eyes I saw
there was no holding him back. So he strips

his coat and in he crawls, and we could hear
to him scraping away among the stones, when
the biggest of the blocks above him settled
down.   He must have moved some of the
small stones inside that upheld it.   And then
there came a groan through the cracks that
sent a grue to our hearts, and we knew that
the great rock was upon him.   We were down
upon our knees and tearing away, till our
hands were bloody and our nails were rent ;
and we got down till we saw the hair on the
head of him, and the big bells of the sweat
that were standing on his forehead.

" ' Can you shift it, Donald ? ' he could just
groan out ; and I would have given ten years
of my life to say ' ay ' to him.   But unless we
had brought half-a-dozen men with bars of
iron, we could never have lifted it one inch.
But when we could say nothing, and he maybe
heard Peter sob—for the fell old hunter was
crying like a woman—all he breathed out was,
' Then the Lord be good to me ! ' and these
were the last words that he ever spoke."

Donald, absorbed in his story, had been
stimulated by Grace's attention.   But when
he looked at her on finishing, her pale face

frightened him. It was not for nothing that
Moray, knowing her impressionable temperament, had been afraid of shocking her by so
tragic a tale. But with her sensitive nerves
she had her father's courage; and it was to the
fate of the unfortunate widow that she turned
her practical mind. She forced Donald to tell
how the news had been "broken" by strong
men who could not control their emotion, and
startled the bereaved widow by the very in-
tensity of their sympathy; and though she
could not go to the cottage in her present agitation, thenceforth her thoughts were full of
its occupant.

Moray was both shocked and angry when
he met the excursionists on their return. His
daughter's nerves had been sadly shaken by
listening to such a narrative so near its scene.
On consideration, it was not difficult to obtain
his forgiveness for Donald, who indeed, in the
circumstances, could hardly have helped speaking. But time after time he cursed his own
folly in letting his daughter go near the churchyard and the cottage. So far as material help
to the widow went, he had nothing with which
to reproach himself. His liberality had fed

and clothed the little family, and was ready to
assure its future into the bargain. But what
haunted Grace, with that slow death-agony
under the boulder, was the look in the widow's
face. There was a touch of the insanity that
brings no oblivion—that distorts the horrors
which memory will revive. Judging by the
effects on herself, a comparatively unconcerned
listener, she could guess how the tragedy must
have told on the woman it so deeply affected.
And with her actively sympathetic nature, in-
action was out of the question. Even her
father, now that the mischief had been done,
felt that she must be left free to follow
her warm impulses. Yet she shrank herself
from approaching so sacred a grief, distrusting
her power of bringing either consolation or
alleviation.

It was then that Leslie had his opportunity
—though, to do him justice, he never thought
of it as an opportunity at the time ; nor did
he know till long afterwards how well he had
improved it. In which he differed altogether
from Mr Venables, who, although perhaps to
the full as warm-hearted as the other, could
never for the life of him help thinking how he

could turn everything to some personal account. There is nothing which a sensible girl
who is vaguely contemplating marriage craves
so much in a lifelong companion as intuitive
sympathy and intelligent affection. They are
the supports on which she hopes to lean—the
shelter that may shield her from the storms of
life. And now Leslie's sympathy, although it
was silent, was as clear to her as the intelligence, the perspicuity of which almost alarmed
her. He said very little, as was his custom,
but she felt that his loving penetration was
searching out her innermost thoughts. And
she knew, besides, and she had good reason
to know, that he was employing himself very
energetically in her service.

When she came down to breakfast, after a
restless night, she had missed her cousin, and
asked about him.

"He called for a glass of rum-and-milk in
his room, and was away by seven o'clock, they
tell me," said her father. "He did not vouch-
safe any message for us, but I fancy we both
guess his business."

So in the early forenoon Grace was saunter-
ing on the path that led over the hills towards

Mrs M'Intyre's shieling. Nor was it long
before she saw Leslie approaching. He was
coming on leisurely, as if lost in thought, but
at sight of her he quickened his pace.

"Well, Ralph!" was all the greeting she
gave him, and yet there was that in her look
and in her tone which amply rewarded him
for his early expedition.

"Yes," he said, answering her unspoken
inquiries—"yes, I have been to see her, and I
think I see, too, how we can help her."

Grace was of course all anxiety; but she
repressed the questions that came crowding to
her lips, leaving her silent cousin to do the
talking. And he spoke with so much good
sense and with such sincere feeling, that she
had never listened to him with greater
pleasure.

"You of all girls will understand me, Grace,
when I tell you that I never was so nervous
in my life as when I walked up to the door of
that poor woman's cottage. There is something so sacred in a calamity like his, that it
seems sacrilege for a man and a stranger to
approach it. And when sorrow has almost
turned the brain, in our ignorance and our

reverence we are almost hopeless to cope with
it. In fact, had it not been for one thing, I
should have gone on hesitating "—he did not
add, " as you have been doing."

But Grace finished the sentence for him in
her mind, and, full of her gratitude, was ready
to reward him.

" And I know what that one thing was, and
that you wished to spare my weakness an
effort. Nor shall I forget it, Ralph—of that
you may be sure; and now tell me everything."

" Really, I don't know that there is much
to tell, except that I have prepared the way
for you, and left her hoping for your visit.
Though that is something, for I am sure you
will do her good, and indeed may probably
prove her salvation. The fact is that the
poor woman has been neglected, though not
intentionally; and mismanaged—with the best
intentions. Your father, as of course he would,
gave his people *carte blanche*, and in the way
of meal, and milk, and mutton, she has everything heart can desire. I believe that the
neighbours, from Donald Ross downwards,
would each one of them cut off a hand to

spare her a finger-ache. But they scarcely
understand her case,—as how should they?
And living in the shadows of that brooding
solitude—you remember our talk of yesterday,
just before we saw her?—her dead is always
with her; the horrors of that death-scene are
always present with her; and I believe, from
what she let slip, that the husband she loved
haunts her in her visions of the night like the
vampires of the Hungarian legends. Unhap-
pily, perhaps, she seems to be a remarkable
woman for her station: what you might have
been," he added, with a serious smile, " had
you been born a shepherd's daughter and
similarly bereaved."

" But the minister?" said Grace. "He is a
good man—is he not? Has he not gone to
visit her?"

"The minister is an excellent man, and his
visits have been only too frequent. From
what I have gathered, and it was a good deal,
his views are as strong and as sincere as they
are narrow. He pities her; he feels for her,
according to his lights; but he is persuaded
that the terrible death was a judgment. And
even in consoling the widow, in his heart and

conscience he feels that he must vindicate the
ways of God to man, and says as much. So
Mrs M'Intyre, believing in her pastor's spir-
itual infallibility, is tormented by the notion
of her husband's doom. If he was made a
flagrant example of the sin of Sabbath-break-
ing — if he was doomed here, he may be
condemned hereafter."

"How terrible!"

"Is it not? But that is just where you
may do unspeakable good, since you can talk
religion as well as common-sense, and speak
to her of mercy instead of judgment. But it
is not for me to tell you, Grace, how you may
best comfort the widow. I should as soon
think of giving a hint to one of the angels: if
you cannot bring consolation to the cottage,
then I throw up my hands. And even the
minister is a candid man, and may listen to
reason and the views of Glenconan's daughter. You go to work with him and with Mrs
M'Intyre, and come to me and report progress.
In the meantime, I wash my hands of the
whole matter — unless, indeed, you should
want money."

"That you assuredly shall not do, or I take

no further step; and I cannot use a stronger threat, for I believe that we *shall* succeed in our errand if we only 'go hand in hand. But you must still be my guide, and, you may be sure, I shall be very docile. Only tell me what I am to do, and you shall have no cause to complain."

Leslie never in his life felt half so happy, and he would have very much liked to have told her so. A community of interests had been established on the highest and holiest grounds; and now he had proved and realised the virtues and the qualities with which he had always desired to credit his cousin. She was worth the loving, and she was worth the living and the working for, so from thenceforth he made up his mind to do both the one and the other; and when Leslie's mind was made up on a subject so all-important, it was by no means easy to move it. That happy moment seriously altered the odds against hopes and ambitions on the part of Mr Venables. And it is more than probable that Grace made a guess at what was passing in his mind; for her colour rose, to her confusion, as her cousin's eyes were riveted on her.

But the confusion passed away, and the community of interest remained. The cousins went like angel-visitors to the cottage, sometimes together, more often separately. They found that the widow could be won to confidences in a *tête-à-tête*, though she would shrink into herself when the two came together. But their sympathy began to teach her acquiescence, which might gradually grow to contented resignation. And although it was not often she spoke the thanks she looked, she could occasionally be eloquent in her gratitude to either when the other was away. She had warm feelings, or she could never have suffered so intensely; and she had been educated above her present station. But let her enlarge on the praises of the absent as she might, she could never tire the patience of either of the listeners. Grace would hear how her manly cousin—who had saved the life of another at the risk of his own, to the admiration of the daring hillmen—could be tender and impassioned as any woman. She heard involuntary comparisons drawn, much to his advantage, between him and the very worthy minister, in whom, nevertheless, as we have said, Mrs

M'Intyre profoundly believed. She admired the tact, though it seemed profanity to call it tact, which he had shown in these delicate circumstances; and reproaching herself for her blindness hitherto, she rather ran into the opposite extreme. In short, she admired him and loved him more and more, and day by day—as a cousin; so it must be confessed that Mr Leslie's chances were looking up.

While as for him, in the true spirit of poetry, he took to idealising the maiden he had longed to adore. Before he thought seriously of loving her, he had been hampered by his distrustful good-sense. He had admired the natural grace of her movements; he had meditated sonnets to her beauties when the fancy seized him; he had liked the liveliness that sparkled in her *badinage* with Venables. But whether it were from a dash of jealousy or doubts as to her depth, he had feared that she and Venables would be fitly matched. For Leslie, with no touch of personal vanity, cherished a good deal of quiet intellectual pride. But with him, as with her, there had come a reaction, and now he was the more ready to worship that he had rashly criticised. Now he figured her to himself as the ministering angel, bringing messages from heaven to desolate hearth; and then, in a natural sequence of ideas, he thought what her presence would be in her husband's home.   Altogether, if Mr Venables had really left his heart in the Highlands, when he went southward full of self-confidence, to study the advancement of his fortunes, he might have had good grounds for uneasiness, had he known all that was going on.

CHAPTER XI.

THE HON. WILFRED WINSTANLEY.

But, come what might of his affair with his cousin, Jack Venables had been doing well for himself. In Winstanley he seemed to have met what the spiritualists would have called his affinity, allowances being made for the difference in their ages. He had succeeded as the other hoped to succeed, by social gifts, by tact, and by enterprise. To be sure, as Jack learned by degrees, Winstanley had had certain advantages in starting. He heard the story bit by bit, and, as it were, incidentally; yet Winstanley was really frank, and willing to be so, for he loved to find an admiring listener. And Jack sat at his feet with unfeigned and flattering interest, storing up the treasures of wisdom which he hoped to turn to practical account.

Mr Winstanley had been the second son of the Viscount Wreckin ; and through his mother he had inherited a handsome independent fortune. Had he been more humbly born and poor, he would probably have done what Jack had dreamed of doing, and turned artist, launching out as an adventurer in full Bohemia. He was fond of art, and had fair talents that way, which possibly he might have cultivated to profitable purpose. He was fond of pleasure too, and it might well have been a question whether art or pleasure would have got the upper hand, had he given himself over to leading the life of a Mürger. As it was, the family traditions kept him straight, and fair play was given to his talents and his ambition. For two or three generations the Winstanleys had been distinguished in public affairs, and they had the habit of intermarrying with the governing Whig families. Taking to politics or diplomacy like ducks to the water, it was only a question with the Hon. Wilfred as to the direction in which he should steer.

He might have sat for a borough which was in reality a close one, though the Winstanley influence was decently ignored. Or he might

try his fortunes in diplomacy, with the absolute certainty that he would be taken care of.
The young aristocrat hardly hesitated. He
had gauged himself and knew that he was
clever, but he was not very sure that he was
profound. He did know that he detested drud-
gery, and he was doubtful whether he might
shine as a speaker. He would as soon have
committed suicide offhand, as condemned
himself to committees and the study of blue-
books; and making a slow reputation as a
hard-working official, seemed a game that was
far from being worth the candle. On the other
hand, diplomacy attracted him. He liked the
idea of looking forward in the future to twist-
ing sultans and kaisers and kings round his
fingers. While in the meantime, with the
strong interest he could command, he might
serve his apprenticeship in pleasant places.

On the whole, he had had little reason to
complain; and if he went through a good deal
of disillusioning, he had the grace to acknowledge that the faults were his own. He was
quick, but not industrious; he was adroit, but
scarcely reliable. He began at Florence as
attaché at the Court of the Grand Duke in

the good old days, and there he made his
reputation as a man who could shine in society, and who was an artistic connoisseur.
He went in for society as matter of business,
and for the fine arts in the way both of business and pleasure. He ran up bills, but he
could afford to pay them; he entertained,
because he liked entertaining, while other
attachés ate at their master's tables, going out
to dinners, and giving none in exchange. So
he early made his mark as a brilliant young
man, who might do the State good service were
he promoted. And even then, his pleasures,
and what apparently were his extravagances,
proved profitable. He flirted freely with maids
and matrons, saying little of importance, and
picking up a good deal. He was the very man
to be set to match some feminine diplomatist,
who, being sent out to shear her dupes, never
dreamed of going home shorn. The ingenuous
youth had a way of looking into women's
eyes, which at once disarmed them and drew
them on. It could hardly be called deceit, it
came so naturally to him. Then his art purchases were even more immediately lucrative
than his social talents. He had grand passions

for particular pictures. There was one Madonna by Correggio, which he bought at what appeared a fancy price, and fitted up in a fancy case, carrying it with him wherever he went. The passion being sated, he sold Our Lady afterwards for cent per cent on the original purchase-money. In fact, although he might be taken in now and then, as must be the fate of the very shrewdest in experience, he generally put out good money at usury, and could realise his investments in the aggregate at a handsome profit.

He married young and for love, which might appear to be inconsistent with his practical character; but, as it chanced, the lady had a considerable fortune, which was subsequently increased by an unexpected inheritance. The lady had likewise a will of her own, as she had a right to have, and we daresay there may have been domestic tussles before she was permitted to indulge it. At any rate, the pair ultimately signed terms of peace, and agreed to go each their own way as they liked, coming together on a footing of friendship when they pleased. Winstanley had gone through all the successive grades, from unpaid

attaché to first secretary of legation ; and then
he became a promising Minister, although he
had never risen to the rank of ambassador.
That, as I said, was very much his own fault.
He was able, but only too versatile, for he
wanted ballast. He loved change of scene,
and was willing to be shifted anywhere, from
the Hague or Frankfort to Quito or Pekin.
And all that could certainly be predicated of
him at the Foreign Office was, that he would
scarcely be settled ere he would wish to change
again. And a change he invariably succeeded
in effecting, which may have gone far to account for his complacent submission, though
he went revolving in secondary spheres in
place of rising to the primary.

So that even in the discharge of his strictly
official duties, the proverb of the rolling stone
could hardly be said to apply to him, for he
rolled out of one good berth into another, and
had always respectable pay and appointments.
But he was a man who had many irons in the
fire, and had a marvellous instinct for never
burning his fingers. As to that, we may let
him speak for himself, as it was a subject on
which he was especially fond of speaking when

he could make sure of his audience. Winstanley detested the semblance of boasting, but he loved sympathetic appreciation. Perhaps it was the unfeigned and only half-conscious flattery of Jack Venables in that respect, which had drawn the elder adventurer most strongly towards the younger one.

Jack had expressed his admiration and astonishment at the number and variety of those irons of Mr Winstanley, though he had merely heard of a few of them in course of conversation.

"Well, you see," said Winstanley, complacently, "I have lived in many places in my time, and have always made it a golden rule to turn my opportunities to the best advantage."

"And such opportunities!" sighingly ejaculated Jack.

"Such opportunities, you may well say. No man can do more in the speculative way than one of her Majesty's diplomatic representatives in foreign parts. The misfortune is, with men sent to Peru or Patagonia, or those sort of places, that very few of them have money. They try to live on their incomes, or to save

upon them, and they fail ignominiously. Now
I had money, as it happened. Trade is forbidden even to consuls now, very properly,
though the poor devils have often to starve
upon a pittance, in obedience to peremptory
though righteous rules.   But a free Briton
may always invest his money in whatever
quarter of the globe he happens to find himself. A diplomatist has always access to the
best information, and should be able to count
on his position for guaranteeing his being
honestly dealt with."

"So, sir?" again ejaculated Jack, hanging
on the lips of the speaker, in the confident
hope of successfully imitating him.

Winstanley was pleased, and went on; perhaps he had his reasons besides.

"Look here, Venables; I have taken a liking
to you, and I don't mind telling you something of my financial story for your guidance.
I owe you a debt, and I hope to do more than
this to pay it; meantime I am sure I may
count on your discretion, for you conceive it
is not to every one that I should give a *cata-
logue raisonné* of my investments."

Jack merely bowed and smiled,—he was too

deeply interested to interrupt; and Winstanley
proceeded :—

"I don't pretend for a moment that the list
is exhaustive; indeed I have been perpetually
selling out and buying again elsewhere, for
even a steady run of gains would pall intoler-
ably. I merely give you some illustrative
cases, and mention what I consider the turn-
ing-points in my career.

"I flatter myself my first hit was an inspir-
ation, and the boldest of all. When in the
Foreign Office as a mere boy, I had made
friends with Isaacs, the great Jew financier;
or rather, Isaacs had condescended to take
notice of me. By way of extraordinary favour, he had allotted me a few shares in the
Universal Bank. The shares had gone up like
balloons, and they came down again as if the
gas was escaping through rents, in the panic
of——I don't precisely remember the year.
I was in mortal terror, for the liability was
unlimited; and I was in blessed ignorance of
the bank's transactions and resources. I rushed
off to my friend Isaacs. I think I must have
taken his fancy, as you have taken mine. It
was after dusk, in his private sitting-room,

and before answering he went to see if the
door was shut, and if the shutters were safe.
Then he came back to me with an air of mystery, and told me that the concern was absolutely safe. 'Schwartzchild' was the only
word he dropped besides, and I could see
that he would shut up like an oyster if I
cross - examined him. I thanked him, and
shook hands, and chewed the cud of medita-
tion through a sleepless night. If I sold, I
should lose seriously, and might possibly be
let in after all. But if the bank was safe,
it must be the time to buy, for the falling
shares were to be had for a song. It was
all a question of Isaacs' good faith, for he
was assuredly in the bank's innermost secrets,
and as to that I exercised my diplomatic perceptions. I was persuaded that the man meant
kindly by me, so I gave commission to sundry
brokers to buy Universal shares. The bank
was smashed up long ago, but I sold all I had
bought afterwards, contenting myself with a
modest gain of £8000. Had I chosen to hold
on, I might have made half as much again;
and had I stuck to the investment, I should
have been a ruined man.

"Those were pleasant times in Paris, when I was second secretary in the Faubourg St Honoré, during the golden days of the Empire. As a member of our Legation, I knew nothing and wished to know nothing of such things as that luckless 'Mexican Question,' which came on later, and was handed over to De Morny for the payment of his debts. But I cultivated M. Haussman and the MM. Fould. I used to dine with those magnificent gentlemen pretty frequently, smoking cigarettes over sweet champagne at dessert, and by putting two and two together, I exercised my prescience, and picked up sundry lots of house property on the lines of the Prefect's projected demolitions.

"I had got rid of most of them before I was sent on to Vienna, to profit by my Parisian experiences in the Kaiserstadt. I had my knife and fork at Schwartzchild's mansion in the Leopoldplatz, and I had my little interest in the house speculations, in the Danube Valley Reclamation schemes and the Hungarian Land-banks. Well, well, perhaps it was lucky for me that the Viennese society and blank days of bear-shooting in the Carpathians bored

me. At all events I was in Pekin, having
cleared out everything Austrian at handsome
profits before the *krach* came in the great
exhibition year. By the way, I remember
that relative of yours, Mr Moray, in China,
but we will talk about him another time. I
soon tired of China, and touched nothing there.
No doubt there was money to be made by out-
siders in silks and opium. But the fact was,
it was the kind of money-making which is
likely to leave pitch on the fingers. And as
I caught an ague besides, I went to sun myself and get rid of the shivers in the dry up-
lands of the Columbian Republic. There I
dipped into coffee-plantations, and dyed my
hands in indigo-growing,—always in the way
of legitimate investments, remember; and I
should have done a good deal better than I
did, had it not been for the moral tone of the
country. I give you my word of honour, that
when you get mixed up with a syndicate there,
the rascals would leave even a British Minister
in the lurch; and more than once I had to
come down handsomely, to save the credit of
those whom malevolent scandal might have
called my confederates. But I pray you to

observe, my young friend, that though I have
made many hits in my time, I never in my
life did one dishonourable action, and so I saw
my properties in Columbia seriously depreci-
ated.   The more was the pity.   Had others
only run as straight, I might have left the
Legation there with a handsome fortune.   And
I don't know, after all, but what I should have
regretted it, for satisfactory speculation is the
salt of life.

"But I am getting prosaic, and I fear I
begin to twaddle.   Oh yes, it is no use your
protesting—I take your civility for what it is
worth.   And at any rate, I should say little
about my squabbles with the Foreign Office.

"As for successive Foreign Secretaries, I
always found them the most impracticable
of men."   And here Mr Winstanley smiled.
"They said—and you may imagine how absurd the accusation was—that I was never to
be counted upon from month to month ; that
the health and digestion which seemed perfect
in London were always breaking down in
foreign climates ; that I was perpetually giving myself leave of absence ; and that if they
sent a specially important despatch, I was

always crossing it *en route.* You conceive, that to a gentleman of comfortable means, there was no dealing with officials of that stamp. So I intimated courteously that, leaving my services at her Majesty's disposal, I was quite content to be shelved in the meantime. To do them justice, they took me readily at my word, offering me the ribbon of St Michael and St George, which I declined respectfully with thanks."

" Did you not find it a little dull, sir, that change to a private life ? "

" Dull, my good friend ! dull ! Why, I am never dull. I have always been too full of occupations. As for being bored sometimes, I don't say : that is a different thing altogether, and the common lot of well-to-do humanity. At this moment I have no end of promising schemes on hand, as you will learn when we improve our acquaintance. But *apropos* to being bored, having a conscience and some consideration for you, I shall ring for my candle, and wish you good night."

CHAPTER XII.

MR VENABLES'S FIRST *COUP.*

WHEN Mr Winstanley walked up-stairs, Mr
Venables strolled off to the smoking-room.
And as he sauntered along the passage, already he was meditating much over his good
friend's autobiographical sketches, and the
useful lessons that had been read to him. He
thought quickly, and already had made up his
mind that much was depending on some
prompt course of action, and that he might
make a great opportunity or miss it. "The
old gentleman likes me ; that is very clear,"—
so ran his reflections ; "and while his gratitude is warm, and we are living almost *en
tête-à-tête*, he would very willingly do anything to help me. Once in London again,
among his many distractions, to say the least
of it, it is quite upon the cards that gratitude

may cool into civility. But if I could only show him that I lay his teaching to heart, if I could make a *coup* on the spot and prove that I might possibly help him, then he would be likely to help me to some purpose, and I might be partner for life in the money-making firm of Winstanley & Venables. Thank heaven, I have that £10,000 to start with! But I am at Oban, and at the back of the world, worse luck, where I have every sort of facility for dreaming, but no chance of doing anything to the purpose." So the sanguine flashes of his ambition died down in momentary despondency, as his fingers were on the handle of the smoking-room door.

Now, as it chanced, the Dunolly Arms Hotel was a rather peculiarly conducted establishment. The season at Oban is brief at the best, so that all the landlords are more or less autocratic. When families of tourists are scrambling for beds, in the fading sunsets of the long summer evenings, they will stoop to any servility to secure them. And necessarily the landlords, who are arbiters of their fates, abuse the advantages of their right of selection. But Mr M'Alpine of the Dunolly Arms was a despot among despots. A benevolent despot, it is true, with a kindly nature at bottom ; but rough of manner and blunt in speech. Like Winstanley, he was an enthusiastic patron of the Fine Arts, and his public rooms and passages were hung with paintings and sketches, many of them of no inconsiderable merit, executed by artists he had entertained and befriended. He paid fair prices, when he did not take paintings in exchange for board and lodgings in the dead season ; he sold these paintings again when he had the chance, and generally got back his money. He could afford to wait for it, as he could afford to lose it. Mr M'Alpine was a small wiry Celt, with a snarl at the corners of the lips, contradicted by a pair of kindly grey eyes, which seemed to say that his bark was worse than his bite. His domestic laws were like those of the Medes and Persians — especially that which forbade tobacco anywhere except in the regular smoking-room. No doubt he knew very well on which side his bread was buttered and, being pecuniarily independent, could afford to persist in a system which remunerated him handsomely in the long-run. And if he showed the wealthy Mr Winstanley a certain consideration, it was more from sympathy with him as a well-known *connoisseur* in the Arts, than from the idea that he might possibly become a purchaser of some of the masterpieces on the walls. Winstanley's valet had been blowing his master's trumpet : Jack Venables was always ready to talk with any one who either amused or instructed him ; and M'Alpine was a well-informed man, with the local knowledge at his finger-ends. Jack had made great way in his good graces by showing him the pocket-book with the clever scratchings of the shipwreck. Old M'Alpine chuckled and criticised ; he laughed especially at a portrait of Mr Winstanley in his ulster, sitting with turned-up trousers in the chair, amid the sea-wrack, the salt water, and the limpets,— a clever study, which, by the way, the sketcher had never submitted to its subject : so that had not Jack been seemingly a gentleman of good estate, M'Alpine would assuredly have given him a commission.

And now Jack had passed the threshold of the door, and was peering through the haze of tobacco-smoke, fragrantly flavoured from beakers of steaming toddy, when the well-known accents of the host welcomed him out of the mist.

" Step this way, Mr Venables ; here's a chair for you, sir." And with unheard-of conde-scension, at which a knot of cronies opened their eyes, M'Alpine rose from the depths of an American rocking-chair and pushed it towards the new-comer. Jack thanked him, protested and accepted, with an easy grace, which brought M'Alpine's allies metaphori-cally to his feet, and perhaps, in a measure, impressed the great man himself. For though nothing could be pleasanter than Mr Venables's manner, somehow he had the knack of keep-ing his inferiors at arm's length, while treat-ing them with encouraging familiarity ; and while swearing he was the best fellow in the world, they would hardly have cared to take a liberty with him.

Jack called for refreshment, and handed round his cigar-case. " Don't let me interrupt you," he said, lying back easily in his chair ; and one of the party, who had been primed with sundry tumblers, took him at his word, and continued the conversation.

Jack sat listening abstractedly, when suddenly he pricked his ears. A burly townsman
was discoursing about sundry land lots, which
he asserted to be going for a song, in the
outskirts of the thriving watering-place.

" I wonder now that you don't make a bid
for them yourself, Mister M'Alpine. The
town is bound to grow ; and ye ken well that
before now, Dunclaverty has been getting £40
—ay, £50—for his feus to the wast. I believe
that these would fetch as much, were you to
bide your time : anyway, if ye got but half
the money, ye'd turn a pretty penny on them.
It's the truth ; and, Mr Baxter, I appeal to
you now, sir ? " addressing himself to the
gentleman next him.

Mr Baxter muttered something that might
pass for an assent ; and even M'Alpine, who
was often contradictory from sheer " cussed-
ness," as the Americans say, did not seriously
dispute the proposition. He contented himself with grumbling that he had more ground
already than he well knew what to do with ;
and that when a man meant to add a wing,
and maybe a stable-yard, to his hotel, it behoved him to see to the balance at his bankers.

And so it chanced that the conversation was changed when Mr Venables had asked some casual questions, apparently more out of politeness than for any better reason.

As a rule, he took things easily in the mornings; but next day he was up and about betimes. Finding M'Alpine admiring his flowerbeds, Jack praised the carnations and picotees, and offered him some rare cuttings from Sussex. Then, easily passing from flowers to shrubs and scenery and land lots, he resumed the talk of the night before to more practical purpose. Subsequently he extended his stroll along the beach, and surveyed certain sunny stretches of the shore, with an eye to house sites and ornamental gardening. He came back with an appetite, and fortified himself with an excellent breakfast. Still indefatigable, he went out again; and was closeted for a couple of hours with a lawyer and bank-agent, who, although he set a very sufficient value on his time, after dragging out title-deeds and plans from sundry tin boxes, insisted on escorting his visitor to the outer door of his office. And a little later, Mr Venables, with the *dégagé* air that sat so naturally on him, strolled into the private sitting-room, in which the companion of his travels was dawdling over a late French breakfast. After a few observations, of course, he went straight to his point.

"And now, sir, if it won't interfere with your digestion, I have come to you for a piece of advice. The fact is, I am thinking of transacting a bit of business, and no one can counsel me better than you."

"Spoil my digestion! Quite the contrary. There is something refreshing in the sound of business, when weeks of idleness are ending in *ennui*—or would have ended in *ennui*, at least, had it not been for your charity and good company. Really, you excite my curiosity besides. What business can you possibly have to transact in this place? For when you were kind enough to tell me all about your affairs the other day, I thought we agreed that the investment of that money of yours was to stand over for our future consideration."

Jack liked the sound of the "our"; it was pleasantly suggestive of the speculative partnership he was contemplating.

"So we did, sir, and so I had intended.

But chances will turn up, as you know, in strange places; and something suggested itself last night, which I have been inquiring into this morning."

Then he told his tale, and produced the memorable pocket-book. There were some figures in pencil on one of the pages, which Winstanley examined with considerable interest, and which were the summing-up of the case that Jack submitted.

"It looks well on paper, I must confess," said Winstanley. "But of course all depends on prospective value; and you are locking up your money, remember that. But 'always distrust a vendor' is a golden rule. Why does this Mr Campbell, your lawyer's principal, wish to sell? He should know the worth of his prospects as well as anybody."

"It is not he, it is his creditors. They are getting impatient for their money, and decline to wait any longer. And M'Alpine and the other men last night, who never dreamed of me as a possible purchaser, agreed that there was no one on the spot with cash ready to pay down. If things are as straightforward as they seem, it appears to me that I can lose nothing,

and may make a good deal. I should borrow
a part of the purchase-money on mortgage,
and merely pay down the difference. My
lawyer friend undertook to have all that arranged for me. And then I see no sort of
reason why I should not develop the property
at once on a considerable scale. They are
shrewd enough here, but scarcely speculative.
Why not launch an Esplanade and Hydro-
pathic Company?—with a palace crowning
that promontory there, and standing in its
terraced gardens. You know something of the
views from the windows, and how one might
make them tell in the prospectus. The land-
locked bay, with the shipping riding at anchor;
the rugged cliffs of Kerrera; the emerald ver-
dure of Lismore; the giant mountains of Glen
Etive and the Land of Lorne looking down on
the lochs that lie sleeping in their shadows,—
I see it all, sir; don't you?"

"Hum! perhaps!" ejaculated Winstanley,
doubtfully. But it struck Mr Jack that he
objected for form's sake, and that he was
inclined to listen to the voice of the charmer.

"Getting out a good Company, and arrang-
ing the preliminary terms so as to make certain

of a fair profit on the launch, is confoundedly
delicate work, my young friend. You may
believe a man who has had some experience
of Company-making."

"No doubt, sir. But that is just where a
few hints from your experience would be in-
valuable, and I don't think you will grudge
me them."

"But, my good friend, you don't think of
doing all that sort of thing yourself,—with
your £10,000, and—excuse me—with your
inexperience ?"

"I have hardly had time to think about it
as yet ; and if I decide that I am hardly likely
to be out of pocket in any case, the first thing
to be done is to secure the property. I have
my reasons for risking something. After all,
if I lose, I am no worse off than I was a few
weeks ago ; if I win, why—not but what I
shall count the chances carefully. I believe,
for example, that if I saw my way, my uncle
Moray, who is rich, would be ready and willing to stand by me. I was loath to apply to
him *in forma pauperis*, but I should be glad
to ask his support in a promising speculation.
Nor do I despair of enlisting our worthy land-

lord; and let me tell you, that M'Alpine would be a veritable tower of strength in Oban here, where his foot is on his native heath. As for you, sir, you have already promised me your advice; so you see that the betting may possibly be in my favour."

Winstanley drummed reflectively on the table with his fingers; then he got up and walked to the window, which commanded a view of those picturesque slopes in which Jack Venables proposed to sink his capital.

"It is certainly a magnificent landscape," he observed, reflectively; "and the air and the ozone, and all that, ought to be of prime quality."

Jack, for his part, was musing aloud. " I can't conceive why that angle of the estate to the back of the railway station has not been bought long before now by the Company. They *must* want it sooner or later. It is the very place for a wharf over the deep water, with rails laid down for landing sheep and cattle. I should never sell it outright for a penny under £4000."

In a moment or two Winstanley turned round abruptly.

"Do you think that lawyer acquaintance of yours will be at home?"

"Sure to be, sir, I should say. He dines at two—so he informed me; and now it is barely one."

"Then, if you don't mind, and as you have done me the honour of consulting me, we will walk along and have another interview. There are one or two points which, for your sake, I should be glad to have cleared up."

The lawyer never dined at two that day. He was persuaded to join the English gentlemen in their private sitting-room at 7.30, at the Dunolly Arms. When he had gone, his gracious host seemed somewhat embarrassed and preoccupied. So much so, that Mr Venables, feeling puzzled and ill at ease, proposed to say good night, and go down to the smoking-room. But when he rose and held out his hand, Winstanley motioned him back to his seat. He was graver than was his wont, yet there was no mistaking the kindness of his manner. As for Jack, his heart beat quicker than usual: he felt there was something serious to be mooted.

Winstanley hummed and hesitated; then

he spoke abruptly, like a man ashamed of his
hesitation, and resolved, at some risk of misconstruction, to put matters on a straightforward footing.

" You know I like you, Venables ; you know
I am indebted to you for a great service ; and
you know that I fully intended to help you.
And I believe you like me quite well enough
to be willing to accept any service I could
offer you. But, to own the truth, you have
been rather too quick for me. You've forced
my hand in a manner. As for this scheme
of yours—to be candid—I think it both a
wise and a foolish one. There's money to be
made, almost to a certainty—by a man who
had money to spare and could afford to watch
his opportunities. Indeed I am so far con-
vinced of that, that I mean to make you a
proposal. But on the other hand, speculation
is speculation ; and those pretty ideas of yours
are intensely speculative, for a fellow with a
mere trifle of capital. No man in your position can promote companies profitably—to his
own advantage, that is to say—for the pikes
will swallow the minnows. And at best, it
would be absolute folly in the circumstances

putting all your eggs into this one basket. Now I daresay that, in the brilliancy of your speculative genius, you think you are carrying your eggs to a golden market, and might distrust any one who volunteered to share the venture."

Jack made a gesture of eloquent negation.

"Oh yes—you may protest; but whatever may be your opinion now, be sure that your second thoughts would be suspicious. I have more than hinted my fears of misconstruction, and now I shall speak out what is in my mind. You have had a happy thought about those Oban land lots, and I should be sorry to see them slip through your fingers. I am far from saying that with money sufficient and with patience, those dreams of yours may not be realised. But believe me, that I think I am doing you a real service, instead of robbing you of legitimate gains, when I frankly offer to share the venture. Take what proportion you will, and leave me the remainder. I may add," and here Winstanley threw significance into the words, " that you shall be no loser by accepting my offer."

Knowing, as we do know, Jack's sanguine

temperament and secret mind, I need scarcely
say that when his elderly friend had finished
the formal speech, he scarcely knew whether
he was sitting in a chair or balancing himself
on the back. In the course of twenty-four
hours his suddenly inspired *coup* had succeeded
beyond his utmost hopes. Come what might
of this Oban affair—and he firmly believed in
it—the solidarity of Winstanley & Venables
had become a reality. He fancied he might
carry those sprats of his to a good market in
Oban; but in any case, with ordinary good-
fortune, his future was assured. He saw a
career of successful speculation before him :
he might propose to his cousin Grace when
next he met her ; and if it were arranged that
they must wait for a year or two, why, he was
content to be patient. Now that marriage
seemed well within his reach, he was persuaded that he was deeply in love with his
cousin ; but then, when doubts and fears are
changing into certainties, there is delight in
dallying with coming felicity. As for Leslie's
rivalry, time might have worked in favour of
that gentleman ; but promptitude on his own
part would nip any of the hopes that Leslie

could scarcely have begun to cherish. So thinking, he gradually composed himself; and then, by a natural association of ideas, he remembered Moray's offers of introductions in China.

Naturally, in his mood of confidence, he reminded Winstanley of them. Now Winstanley, like Jack, was essentially a man of impulse, and of single ideas on which he would concentrate for the time the full flashes of his intelligence. He was thinking of indulging the luxury of gratitude, and forwarding the views of this young man, who would be a creditable and profitable *protégé*. He dreamed of playing the game of ambition at second-hand in his decline, and using both political and financial influence in Venables's favour. So, as was sometimes a habit of his, he thought aloud, and said—

" My dear boy, your going out to the East would be a mistake. You will do a great deal better at home, to say nothing of living in place of existing."

Before the words were well out of his lips, Jack Venables had thanked him with unfeigned gratitude; and grasping his hand with

a pressure that clenched the alliance, had
effected his escape into the open air. And
although Jack had acted for once without the
slightest *arrière-pensée*, he could scarcely have
played his cards better. He wanted to be
alone and to think ; to revel in the prospects
brightening before him ; to walk himself off
his legs in the sea-air, and relieve the lungs
that seemed to be overcharged. While Winstanley, left to his solitary reflections, realised
the responsibility he had accepted. In step-
ping between this lad and his wealthy uncle—
in setting down his foot on a scheme which
promised ultimate wealth—he had virtually
charged himself with the care of his future.
So that, after all, it was well he could say to
himself in sincerity that he by no means regretted what he had done, although somewhat
ashamed of having so hastily committed himself beyond honourable retractation.

CHAPTER XIII.

MORAY GOES INTO THE CONFESSIONAL.

LEAVING Winstanley and his young companion to continue their journey to the south, where we shall meet them again ere many months are over, we return to the inmates of Glenconan. Moray had made all the arrangements for the round of visits of which he had spoken to his nephew; and it must be confessed that Grace was looking forward to them with pleasure. She might be " a perfect woman nobly planned," as Leslie thought, and had once ventured to tell her. But she was not a bit "too good for human nature's daily food," and he was very glad to think so. She knew very well she was attractive, and she loved to make herself agreeable. Though no coquette, she did not disdain conquests—what girl who is worth her salt ever did? As yet she had really seen nothing of society, and she was willing enough to make preparations for the coming campaign. Her cousin Jack, though no ascetic in a general way, would probably have disapproved her correspondence with Madame Antoinette of Bond Street, and cut down the orders for costumes. The dazzling visions his artistic imagination would have conjured up, of virgin beauty in billowy white, like a purer Cytherean Venus rising from the sea-foam, were not to be for him. As for Leslie, who never gave his confidence by halves, characteristically he trusted the sweet refinement of her taste, and was pleased with anything that gave her pleasure. Were she ever to be his wife—and perhaps Grace felt that in such trifles more than in graver things—he would assuredly be at once the most trustful and generous of husbands. Not that as yet there was anything in the least serious between them : but a girl like Grace, of course, will have her dreams—especially in such solitudes as those of Glenconan ; and when her fancy peopled some future home, now she might occasionally think of Leslie as its master.

Grace's interest in her toilets was very natural, and Leslie looked on and listened benevolently when she was reading notes written to London aloud to her father; nay, he even volunteered suggestions as to garnitures and trimmings, which were generally more poetical than practical. But Moray's behaviour puzzled him : it seemed so strangely inconsistent. He knew his uncle to be one of the most liberal of men ; it was certain that he doated on his only daughter. He had given her *carte blanche* to send for what she pleased—for, like Leslie, he had confidence in her taste and discretion ; and yet it appeared to the young man that he sometimes actually grudged her things. It was a metaphysical problem that Leslie was curious to solve, for he did not like to feel anything but respect for his uncle ; and had Venables been there to talk with, he might have enlisted his shrewdness in attempting to come to a satisfactory conclusion.

"My uncle," he said to himself, "is a man of sense and firmness ; and if he wished his daughter to be extremely simply dressed, he would say so frankly. But I am sure there is nothing of that in his mind; and indeed, if it were left to him, with his gorgeous oriental reminiscences, I believe he would be inclined to over-dress her. I remember how, much against her will, he made her come down one evening in cashmeres, and sparkling in his mother's diamonds. He is proud of her looks, as he well may be, and proud of her position as the heiress of Glenconan. That he is willing, with it all, to let her marry modestly, I can understand, for he seeks to assure her happiness before all things. And as he likes to see her happy, he tries hard to seem pleased when she is laughingly making much ado over one of those letters to the dressmakers. Could she see the cloud that overcasts his face the next moment, my word for it, that letter would never be sent. For once in their lives the two misunderstood each other; and I should be glad to get at the bottom of the mystery."

Had it been Jack Venables, he would have marked and inwardly observed, without letting his uncle suspect anything. But Leslie was more deeply absorbed where he was interested: he gave far less thought to appearances; and

more than once his uncle caught his steady
and inquisitive gaze, while Leslie's obvious
embarrassment, with an awkward habit of colouring up, emphasised the scrutiny somewhat
unpleasantly. Moray, as we know, was frank
to a fault, and, moreover, on the most friendly
terms with his nephew, and he justly appreciated his judgment and character. Besides, he
longed for a confidant; and being eager to
relieve his mind, was screwed up to the ex-
planatory point by his nephew's approaching
departure. So it came about that one evening
when Grace had gone to bed, he broached his
subject and dashed into the middle of things.
He laid his hand on the young man's shoulder,
and looked wistfully into his kindly eyes as
if seeking for the sympathy he was sure to
find.

"I have been occupying you a good deal
lately, Master Ralph, and you are beginning
to think you may have been mistaken in me."

"Not that, sir, believe me. But since you
ask me, I may own that I see there is a mystery; and I should be very glad to have it
cleared away, for many reasons, and as much
for my cousin's sake as my own."

" That is the very reason why I have spoken. Cleared away the mystery shall be, and I have been longing to make a clean breast of it. Grace is more deeply concerned than myself; and I have sometimes thought she would be my safest counsellor. But then, as yet she knows nothing of the world; and the more innocent a woman is, the more certainly she will be swayed by the spirit of self-sacrifice and an over-sensitive generosity. Now you, although you are young, are enough of a man of the world to understand me; and you have been living long enough under my roof to make me recognise you for the soul of honour."

Leslie merely bowed. He was too much interested to interrupt; and after all, his conscience told him that his uncle only did him justice.

" To say the honest truth, if I have hesitated so long, it is because I feared you would pronounce in favour of my scruples; and then there would be a change in our circumstances —in Grace's future."

He paused, as if expecting Leslie to speak. But Leslie, all in the dark, did not know what to think. What he did say was, " I presume

you mean that your fortune is somehow compromised; but I fancied it had all been satisfactorily invested."

"So far as I know, my fortune is safe
enough; certainly it is large enough. The
most speculative of the investments are in
sound bank-stocks. No; I may call myself
a wealthy man, and that is precisely the cause
of my trouble. You stare, as well you may;
and yet I assure you I am to be pitied. There
has been a cloud cast over my cheerfulness
ever since I came back from the East, with
money enough to clear Glenconan and leave
my girl a wealthy heiress. Do you remember
that drive of ours from the railway station to
the house, when you and Venables came north
with me? I don't know whether you chanced
to remark anything, but he was quick enough
to suspect. I have seldom looked forward to
anything more than to that return to my
family home, with the feeling that I had re-
trieved the family fortunes. It was like leaving the fevers of the jungles for the fresh air
of the Highland hills; it was the beginning
of a new life among the grouse and the deer,
in the wild picturesqueness of my native glens.

Yet a skeleton was sitting in the carriage, by way of bodkin between you and me: in the very moment of triumphant exhilaration, I seemed to hear the rattle of the bones. Talk of skeletons in cupboards: I suppose you may lock them away and forget them for a time. But as for mine, it has always been with me, more or less, of late; and as the hope that it would cease to haunt me dies away, I begin to think that something must be done to get rid of it."

Leslie was fairly taken aback: he sat in his chair, silent and expectant. He had made sure that his uncle had a trouble, but he had suspected nothing so serious as this. In the man who seemed moved from all his habitual self-restraint, and nerving himself to lay bare his innermost secrets, he scarcely recognised the cheery and well-preserved old Highlander, whose spirits should have been as equable as his digestion was sound. Surely his uncle must be the prey to some mad hallucination; for it was impossible to believe he had reason to be the victim of remorse. But whether it were really remorse or a hallucination was the question he was presently to be asked to decide.

There is no need to go into all the details of Moray's disclosures. Infinite worry as his mental anxieties had caused him, it was but a question of conscience or of casuistry, after all, and it lay in a nutshell. The first of the revelations that surprised Leslie was, that the imperturbable composure of manner, which seemed to match so well with a constitution of iron, masked a temperament almost morbidly sensitive. Making a plunge into the confessional, Moray had opened the conversation abruptly.

" I said, a moment ago, that I considered you the soul of honour : frankly, and without compliments, what should you have said of me ? "

" Why, surely, sir, the question is strangely unnecessary. I would stake my life and my own honour upon yours."

" I thought as much ; and I do not say you are wrong. For many a long year I have never knowingly been guilty of an act with which I can reproach myself ; and if I knew I had unwittingly injured any man, I would willingly make him restitution fourfold."

" I am persuaded of it, sir,—and so much

so, that if you will forgive my impatience,
I entreat of you to come to the point."

For Leslie, thinking of Grace, knew not
what to imagine, and was inclined to fear the
worst. He might be a fool, but was it possible that the life of his placid uncle could
hide one of those terrible secrets or scandalous
hypocrisies which one reads of in sensational
novels, or in more sensational criminal trials?
He must be a fool, and such a supposition
was out of the question; but in that case his
uncle was the victim of morbid insanity—and
if so, it was scarcely better for Grace.

But Moray, speaking faster than was his
habit, proceeded speedily to set his nephew's
mind at ease.

The long and the short of the story was,
that his conscience pricked him as to the be-
ginnings of his fortune. And as the constant
dropping of water will wear away a stone, so
with that perpetual pricking his conscience
had become ulcerated.

"I was young and poor when I went out to
the East,—young and poor, adventurous and
thoughtless. That is to say, I thought enough,
when it was a question of devising and carry-

ing out some hazardous but lucrative combination. But I thought of the end and of the means to it, and not of their manner or their morality. There is much to be said in extenuation, I know; but extenuation at best infers culpability. The tone of mercantile society was free and easy in the Chinese seaports; in the Straits Settlements, and in the Malay territories, the morality of the European traders was still more lax. I did nothing that was not heartily approved by the representatives of our leading houses in China; my best strokes of business were suggested by men whose names have always stood above reproach. One success led on to another, and I was flattered by the praise bestowed on my lucky ventures. Gradually I shook myself loose from more questionable schemes, and launched out in strictly legitimate trade. But I can never forget that the best of my early hits were flagrant breaches of the Chinese revenue laws,—that I followed them up by certain trading transactions with Malay rajahs, which I scarcely think now would bear close investigation. I was no worse than anybody else; indeed I may say I was much better than

many, for I had always my code of honour—
and although it might be elastic, I strictly
obeyed it.   No, I can never reproach myself
with knowingly acting dishonourably.   But all
the same, as I see things now, I doubt if I
ought to have made the *coups* which began to
enrich me.   And now, Ralph, what do you
say of it all?"

I have condensed a prolix explanation into
a few brief sentences.   Leslie could not help
admiring the frankness with which his uncle
made what was evidently a most trying confession.   Yet it pained him to see the resolute
man, who was in the habit of expressing
opinions briefly and decidedly, as if they
scarcely admitted a rejoinder, pleading hard
for the lenient judgment which might salve
his conscience and reconcile him to himself.
He was touched when Moray added, very unnecessarily, "Of course you will not breathe
a whisper of this to Grace."   He would have
given much to have been able to speak offhand
with such obvious conviction that his answer
must have carried immediate comfort; but he
could not collect himself sufficiently for that,
and indeed he hardly knew what to say.   The

soul of honour, as his uncle had said, he had not lived in the Anglo-Chinese colonies five-and-twenty years before, nor could he put himself in so unfamiliar a position at a moment's notice. For himself, he would have been sorry to have made his money by running opium, or by stretching points with semi-barbarians, even though these enterprises had left him with a fortune which would have entitled him to ask for his cousin straightway. Yet, on the other hand, he was so anxious to soothe his uncle's susceptibilities, that in giving an answer he rather compromised with his conscience. As happens generally when we weakly steer a middle course, the trimming was unsatisfactory to both. Ralph said, somewhat hesitatingly, that as Moray had always acted for the best, he ought not to reproach himself with any peccadilloes he had committed; that the invariable and unimpeachable purity of his subsequent conduct should be a guarantee for his having acted with honourable intentions. Moray listened sadly, and shook his head. The answer did not give him the comfort he had hoped, and his excessive sensitiveness read between the lines, imagining more than was passing in his nephew's mind, and ignoring the difficulties that beset this young Daniel, called so suddenly to judgment. Naturally they talked on, going over and over the same ground,—till Leslie was really converted or persuaded into saying much that Moray would have had him say at the first. At least he warmed up so far as to declare that he thought his senior's scruples were rather fantastic ; that, at all events, he could hardly make restitution to the Government or the rajahs he fancied he might have wronged ; and that he might set his mind at ease if he made a good use of his money.

"Ay, there it is !" said Moray. " It has often occurred to me that I might anticipate my death, and give away the bulk of my wealth in charity, or for philanthropical objects ; though, having worked hard and cleared Glenconan, I confess I should like Grace to have that—and I think she honestly might in any case. But what merit would there be in so far impoverishing myself? If anybody were to suffer, it would be Grace, who would suffer vicariously. As for me, give me a quiet life here in the Highlands, and I should ask

nothing better. But this is where the shoe
pinches. If the money were fairly made, it is
Grace's as much as mine; and if I part with
it, I am easing my conscience at her expense,
—which, as you must admit, would be both
unmanly and dishonest. On the other hand,
if I have really enriched myself by faults—
not to say frauds—I ought to make restitution
somehow and *coûte que coûte.*"

"Precisely so," said Leslie; "but you have
repeatedly used the word 'restitution,' and it
appears to me to help us out of the dilemma.
Supposing — I say, that supposing you are
right in reproaching yourself, nevertheless
you cannot restore your gains to the rightful
claimants. I cannot imagine any conceivable
way in which you could rationally set about
it. It follows, then, that you must keep your
money, turn it to useful purposes while you
live, and leave it behind you with a clear
conscience to a child who is sure to follow in
your footsteps."

"And that piece of advice," he thought, as
he gave it, "is thoroughly disinterested; for
it leaves obstacles in my way that might
otherwise be removed. If Grace were to be

poor, or only moderately rich, I think I should venture to try my fortunes with her on the moment."

Nor did Moray appear to be much better satisfied.

"I have a foreboding all the same," he remarked, dejectedly, "that if I do as you suggest, or, in other words, do nothing, the matter will be taken out of my hands, and the difficulty before long will settle itself. And for myself, I cannot say I should be sorry. I think that all my investments are safe and solid; yet, mark my words, you will see that money slip through my fingers." Then, as if ashamed of himself and his superstition, he tried to give the conversation a brighter turn—not very successfully. "You know, my foster-mother came of a family that had the second-sight; and possibly she may have communicated the gift to her nursling."

Then, after a few moments' silence, he spoke abruptly and like his ordinary self, as if he had taken a resolution and was determined to act upon it.

"I shall rent a house in London for a year, from the end of the autumn. Grace must be introduced, and should go to a Drawing-room next spring; and .she may as well pass the winter in town. I trust we shall see you there : there are sure to be plenty of spare bedrooms."

Whereupon, without waiting for a reply, he shook hands, and walked out of the room, leaving his nephew to very grave reflections.

CHAPTER XIV.

MR AND MISS MORAY "COME OUT."

NINE months are supposed to have elapsed, as they say in the play-bills. It is early spring in London, and drawing on towards the beginning of the season. The Morays are very comfortably established in a moderate-sized mansion in Eaton Place. Glenconan had thought of renting a house, but subsequently he had changed his views. He had listened to the words of worldly wisdom as they fell from the lips of Lady Fortrose,—a far-away Highland cousin, and a very *grande dame*. The Morays, having gone to Fortrose Castle on a visit of a few days the year before, had passed nearly a month under that hospitable roof. Her ladyship had taken a fancy to Grace ; his lordship and Moray had much in common. Lady Fortrose having married a

pair of pretty daughters, had her time much
at her own disposal, and welcomed a new
interest. She admired Grace as much as she
liked her, and felt she would be a very desirable *protégée.* And if it pleased her to take a
young lady by the hand, it was everything to
the girl from a social point of view. She had
more than the *entrée* to the best society; ad-
mission to her house was coveted by everybody save the few who came there as a matter
of course. It opened the gates of possible
paradises to marriageable young women, for
she only welcomed those who were attractive,
and she always managed to have the best
men. Lord Fortrose was an English baron
as well as a Scottish earl; and though he
spoke but seldom and shortly in the House,
he had always carried a certain weight in
politics. He had collieries in Durham and
coverts in Kent, as well as his famous forest
in Perthshire; his French cook had taken
honours in the imperial kitchens at Berlin,
as the most promising *élève* of Urbain Dubois;
and his cellars, both in the country and in
town, were celebrated for their well-selected
contents. So my lord's little dinners in Bel-

grave Square launched wealthy young *viveurs* into her ladyship's small receptions, in the mood to be soothed by soft music and won by the witcheries of beauty to wise indiscretions. And Lady Fortrose, with all her inclinations to worldliness, was really a worthy woman and a reliable chaperon. No wonder, then, that Moray had met her advances more than half-way, and was willing to listen to her advice. His motherless daughter could have no better friend.

He had written to London agents about houses, and one of them chanced to mention the mansion in Eaton Place. Mr Moray, he knew, had not intended to purchase; but possibly, under the circumstances, he might be tempted. The proprietor had suddenly died, and his heir had given instructions to dispose of it. It was newly and handsomely furnished and fitted up: decorations by Trollope, furnishing by Gillow; and all in good and simple style. A moderate price would be accepted for money down; and the agent could recommend it as a safe investment.

Moray mentioned the matter to Lady Fortrose. She exerted herself about it in the

most flattering manner! "Really, my dear
Mr Moray, it seems a special interposition of
Providence. Your house and ours will be
within easy distance of each other : Grace can
run across at any time, with the footman or
even with her maid ; and I can always pick
her up of an evening, without going any distance out of my way. If it were only for my
sake, you must not hesitate. You must write
—or better, telegraph at once."

Moray did not telegraph, but he bought the
house ; and hitherto he had no cause to regret
the purchase. Lady Fortrose grew more affectionate and more motherly every day; her
husband was almost as fond of Grace as she
was : and so the girl had a couple of homes,
and perhaps more gaiety than was good for
her. She went out shopping with her ladyship in the brougham of a morning; she went
visiting with her, or into the Park, in the
barouche of an afternoon. On fine days she
rode out under his lordship's escort when her
father was not inclined to get on horseback ;
and she might have had any number of en-
gagements in the evenings, but that she often
insisted on staying at home and keeping him

company. As for Moray, he enjoyed the town
life but moderately. He had his clubs, to
which he had been elected years before, on his
occasional visits to England. He had his
cronies, chiefly from the Highlands or the
East—though, being essentially a man of the
world, he made acquaintances in many circles.
There was society enough at the house in
Eaton Place, where the dinners were very
sufficiently well served, if less *recherché* than
Lord Fortrose's. He often rode out with his
daughter; he sometimes went in for a day's
golfing at Wimbledon. But all the same, the
existence dragged, and would have been still
more wearisome had it not been for two unselfish sources of pleasure. The one was seeing his daughter happy; the other, his indulging himself—for indulgence it was—in many
an action of generous philanthropy. The
memorable conversation with Leslie had borne
fruit in one way if not in another. He had
not made public expiation by sacrificing his
fortune, but he practised liberality on an
almost prodigal scale. He not only drew
handsome cheques for estimable charities, but
he never spared himself; and he mortified the

flesh as much as he indulged it. He had a
vigorous constitution and an excellent appetite; he was much more inclined to be a *bon
vivant* than an ascetic; and when he gave
dinner-parties at home or dined with other
people, he always set his friends a good example. But after the coffee and cigars, he would
slip away; or he would charter a cab after
breakfast next morning, and drive off to the
Surrey side or the Borough, or to the poverty-
stricken purlieus of eastern London. He had
struck up an intimacy with sundry hard-working and self-sacrificing clergymen, who knew
they might always draw on his purse. He
had munificently subsidised certain police in-
spectors, who were ever ready to give him
their company or an escort at the shortest
notice. But indeed he had come to be tolerably well known himself in some of the worst
of the warrens and most squalid of the rook-
eries; and he was known for a man who could
take his own part, as he was far from being
pharisaical as to publicans and sinners. More
than once he had been hustled on a dark stair-
case, when the assailants had felt the iron
muscles of a man who was more than a match

for half-a-dozen of them. But then he would distribute shillings in place of soup-tickets, and seldom asked for a voucher from the charity organisation society before putting his hand in his pocket. "Probably," he would tell himself, "the poor wretch is lying. Certainly ninepence out of my shilling will be spent in the gin-palace at the corner—and what then? If he gets himself a loaf, I shall have done a good action; and as for the liquor, that is his look-out. It is something to forget one's misery for five minutes; and if I had as reasonable an excuse for my own mistakes or misconduct—why, perhaps I might be justified in throwing stones at him."

So, while his friends agreed that Moray was odd, upon the whole they liked and admired him for his "eccentricities." The more so, that he left rumour to blow his trumpet, never letting his left hand know what his right hand was doing, and only making a confidant of his daughter—for from her he could keep no secrets.

CHAPTER XV.

VENABLES AND LESLIE TALK THINGS OVER.

LESLIE and Venables were both in town, and Grace saw a great deal of her cousins. Moray's house was always open to them; and they "drew him," as Jack phrased it, very freely for luncheon, and not unfrequently for dinner. Leslie, who loved to be independent, had declined his uncle's offer of a bedroom, and established himself in apartments in Jermyn Street, where he was said to have become a slave of the lamp. Though he rose early and took a constitutional before breakfast, after coming home from dining out or at his club, he was in the habit of sitting up to most unchristian hours; and his friendly landlady took Miss Moray into her confidence, expressing heartfelt anxiety as to his health. The young man looked pale, though perhaps his

handsome face was all the more interesting
for that. But his friends, and Grace in
particular, found him changed otherwise, and
considerably to his advantage. Quiet and
rather prematurely dignified in manner as he
always was, he was more easily moved now
from his constitutional apathy. There was a
sparkle in his hazel eyes which would break
out in flashes of flame on any subject that
interested him; and more frequently than
before, as he warmed, he would forget himself
and become winningly eloquent. He had
good introductions and connections, and
already he began to make his mark. He
was a welcome guest at many a dinner-table.
Men of station and high reputation listened
to him respectfully—for when he spoke he
always spoke to the purpose; and there was
a certain poetical originality in his talk, with
a quaint and fanciful humour. Grace watched
him curiously and with cousinly regard.
Womanlike, she admired him more, that
others evidently admired him. Now there
was apparently some purpose in his life. He
seemed to see his way, and to have hopes
rather than aspirations. And from what she

knew of him, she was persuaded that he
would go forward with determination toward
his determined point, whatever that might be.

As for Jack Venables, there was less doubt
as to his prospects. Unlike Leslie, he made
no secret of his aims, which indeed were
sufficiently obvious. Jack had lighted on his
legs, and was making the most of his chances;
and it was well for him that it was so.
Steady disappointments or a run of ill-luck
might have crippled him, as cold paralyses
the constitution of a creole. But with the
feeling that Fortune was patting him on the
back, he played card after card with cool
audacity, and brightened in the smiles in
which he basked. Fortune might pet but she
did not spoil him, and he bore his honours,
such as they were, so modestly that nobody
envied him his luck. It was Winstanley who
had dealt him his trumps, taking a fatherly
pride in him, and standing sponsor to him
in society. Winstanley had done for him
more than Lady Fortrose for Grace. He
could hardly have happened on a more
efficient patron, for Winstanley was welcome
wherever he went, knew everybody who was

worth the knowing, and had opportunities of doing good turns to so many men, that many men were ready to fawn upon his friend. And Jack was more than a friend : he was the son of the house ; he was become a connecting-link between its master and its mistress, for he had carried the heart of Mrs Winstanley on a first introduction. Jack, who ought to have known best, and whose worst enemies could not have taxed him with any want of candour when it was a question of talking confidentially to friends, had explained the situation to Leslie, shortly after Leslie's arrival in town. Possibly he may have spoken a little boastfully, but for that we may make due deduction.

"Well, Jack, I presume your career is fixed now, and you mean to blossom out a full-blown financier ? "

"Financier—financier,—that depends how you understand the word. If you mean a professional money - maker who thinks of nothing else, you never were much wider of the mark. If you mean that I hope to be like one of the financiers of the old French *régime*, who ground the helpless in their hardness, that in their ostentation they might be *écrasé* by the *noblesse*, you never were more mistaken in your life. A man who goes in for mere money-making is contemptible. Besides, I have no fancy for being a cockshy for the curses of the widow and the orphan. I don't care about them. But if you mean that I am likely to have many opportunities of turning legitimate speculations to lucrative account, and if you add that I don't intend to neglect them — there, my boy, you are right."

" Why, Jack, you have turned strangely fiery ; but you need not be so sensitive on the point of honour. Wait till anybody impugns it. I only want to hear how you get on."

" And so you shall, my dear Ralph : I see no reason for being silent ; and you have a right to know everything, even if you were not the very fellow I should naturally come to in a scrape. You helped me out of one already, you may remember. Though I seldom speak of it, I never forget."

" It was you and your affairs we were talking about," rejoined Leslie, hastily. " And

you really like the Winstanleys, and get on
with them ?"

"Like them—yes, I like them all; and as
for the old gentleman himself, he is a trump.
I owe pretty nearly everything to him and
to that shipwreck which I mentioned to you.
My legacy was all very well, and I am most
grateful to the worthy testator; but it is Winstanley who has made it fructify in the meantime, with the hopes of bearing fortyfold fruits
in the future. He has let me in for half-a-
dozen good things already; and each of them
may be a stepping-stone to something better.
It is all a question of getting the preliminary
capital together; then it must go on rolling
up of itself."

" *Ce n'est que le premier pas que coûte;* and
I imagine that initial difficulty has puzzled
many people. However, with your legacy and
your friend, you have so far solved it; so we
may hope the best. And this discriminating
old gentleman has taken a veritable fancy
to you ?"

"To tell the truth, old fellow,—I know it
will go no further, but I love to make a clean
breast when I can,—to tell the truth, it is

something more than a fancy. He overrates
me, I know, but somehow I suit him; and he
appears to take a sort of fatherly pride in me.
In short, he has made me one of his pet speculations, and he is determined the speculation
shall succeed. He has employed me already
in all manner of business, and insists on paying or promising me handsome commissions.
Nor does he ever neglect an opportunity of
pushing me in society; and he has helped me
to any number of useful acquaintances."

"Well, I congratulate you with all my heart
upon your good fortune;" and to do him
justice, Leslie probably meant it, though the
unwelcome thought would flash through his
mind, that this gay, gallant, prosperous young
fellow would surely be a formidable rival with
Grace. And perhaps it was by a natural sequence of ideas that he asked, "And the ladies
of the Winstanley household, how do you
stand with them?"

"Oh, the ladies!" said Jack, laughing; "I
was *au mieux* from the first with both mother
and daughter. Mrs Winstanley wants managing—perhaps her husband, clever diplomatist
as he is, hardly has the knack of it; but she

and I hit it off admirably. The day may come when I may have to choose between the two; and then, of course, gratitude must decide my choice. But in the meantime, Mrs Winstanley and I are the best friends in the world."

"And how is it with the fair Miss Julia, if it be not an indiscreet question?"

"Indiscreet! By no manner of means. Julia is very good-looking,—classical features, pearly complexion, faultless figure, and all the rest of it; she is highly accomplished as well: and of course I admire her, as everybody else does. But she knows, too, that she can never touch my heart; so we are on the easiest possible footing. Then we are allies, though we have never acknowledged it to each other, with common interests and a common object."

"As how, if it please you? You certainly seem to have made the most of your time."

"Why, simply because hitherto it has been Julia's mission to keep the peace between her father and her mother. Perhaps talking of keeping the peace is going too far, because they are too well-bred and too sensible to quarrel. And indeed, I believe Mrs Winstanley to be still in love with her husband, other-

wise she would never bear him a grudge. But
he gave her Art and those speculations of his
for rivals, and she has never forgiven it; nor
was it flattering that 'duty' was always sending him on foreign missions, where the climates did not suit her constitution. She likes
pictures herself, but she will not sympathise
with his buying them. She likes money, and
she spends a deal of it; but she has nothing
to say in favour of his happiest speculations;
and to this day she resents his habit of roving
about the world *en garçon*. Julia assures me
that her mother was in a terrible taking when
she heard of that shipwreck of ours. Yet
when she received the prodigal on his safe
return, she does not seem to have sinned on
the side of tenderness, and she intimated a
verdict of 'serve you right.' No wonder that
a good-tempered but gouty gentleman was
apt to ride rusty in the circumstances. Then
Julia throws oil on the troubled waters; and
the girl has even more than her father's tact."

"That is all very well, so far as the young
lady is concerned, and much to her credit.
But I don't quite understand how Mrs Winstanley should make you welcome in the

house, seeing you go heart and soul into all her husband's schemes."

Jack blushed a little. Perhaps with all his frankness he did not care to declare how "diplomatic" he had been in domestic talks with the lady. But it was not easy to take him aback, and he had a plausible answer.

"Oh, that is easily explained. Mrs Winstanley is a woman of sense, and understands her husband by this time. She knows that he cannot live without his speculations; that to the last day of his life, bar gout in the foot, he would go half across Europe for an 'old master' that tempted him. But if he is not to be weaned from his passion, he may do much of his work by deputy; and she is willing he should adopt me as a sort of roving partner in the concern, as a better kind of commercial traveller in whose discretion he may confide. In that case, she might domesticate and reclaim him, even at the eleventh hour. For, love apart, she feels it anything but gratifying that her husband should show himself almost ostentatiously independent of her. That at least is my theory of her motives, though she has never told me as much in so many words; and you must own the theory is plausible."

"Perhaps so," rejoined Leslie, somewhat dubiously. "Now one other question, and the examination is at an end." But having said so much, he hesitated. For the life of him he could not help the hesitation, though he would have given much to have spoken easily as before.

"Out with it!" said Jack, unsuspiciously.

"How comes it, then, that this man and this woman of the world, with a daughter and heiress both beautiful and rich, throw her into the company of Mr Jack Venables, who is not without his ambitions and his fascinations? It must surely have struck them, if it has not struck you, that Mr Venables might take a short cut to becoming more a member of the family than he has been."

If Leslie hoped that, notwithstanding what he had said before as to his easy footing with Miss Winstanley, Jack would have added something now towards relieving him from the apprehension of any rivalry, he was doomed to disappointment. Jack, in his turn, felt embarrassed—but only for a mo-

ment. After all, he had only to say what
Leslie knew, or ought to have known; and
if he had any doubts, he should have avoided
the subject. So he answered lightly but
decidedly—

"I repaid confidence with confidence. I
was frank with old Winstanley from the first,
and told him of my hopes and my affections.
He knows that I have set my heart on Grace.
Whether she will ever have me, who can say?
In any case, Miss Winstanley is safe, so far
as I am concerned; and her parents are persuaded she may die an old maid, for anything
I should suggest to the contrary."

Whereupon he got up and took his leave;
nor did Leslie make any attempt to detain
him. Jack held that, if anything, he had the
prior claims; and Leslie could only feel that
it was a fair match between them. Down at
Glenconan, Leslie would have said that the
chances were all in his favour. Here, in London, he was by no means so sure. Like most
men of real merit, he set a very modest value
on himself; and in the whirl of society, Grace
seemed to be swept away from him into
spheres whither he scarcely cared to follow

her. Should she be demoralised by fashion-
able company, she would be no mate for him ;
and though he was sure he could never get
over his disappointment, he was not the man
to go chasing a Will-o'-the-wisp. All the
same, he hoped better things : he could not
forget the communion of their spirits over the
case of the forlorn widow in the Highland
glen. And so, with an effort of the will, he
tried to dismiss the subject in the meantime,
turning for doubtful comfort to his books and
the papers that littered the writing-table.

END OF THE FIRST VOLUME.

PRINTED BY WILLIAM BLACKWOOD AND SONS.

RECENT PUBLICATIONS.

THEREBY. By FAYR MADOC. Two Volumes, post 8vo, 17s.

"The work is excellent. 'Thereby' is one of those few works of fiction which come from the pen of the modern novelist which are not simply re-arrangements and repetitions.......The novel is original."—*London Evening News.*

"One of the most thoughtful, and at the same time most amusing and in-teresting, novels issued of late.......Unconventional to a degree in theme, character, and style, it is one of those books which are 'devoured,' and only relinquished with regret."—*Society.*

OAKS AND BIRCHES. By NASEBY, Author of 'Only Three Weeks,' &c. Three Volumes, post 8vo, 25s. 6d.

"It is a really brilliant novel.......The great interest of the novel is wrought with unusual skill and power out of that dominating idea."—*Saturday Review.*

AN ILL-REGULATED MIND. By KATHARINE WYLDE, Author of 'A Dreamer.' Crown 8vo, 7s. 6d.

"The tale is a sweet, pitiful, perhaps somewhat slight and fanciful, work of imagination, not without the loveliness of genius illuminating it."—*Scotsman.*

"The tale is told in quaint, pretty fashion, full of peculiar charm."—*St James's Gazette.*

"The special merit of this tale is the study of one of the female characters. ......A story which contains one such study as this must be ranked above the average."—*Pall Mall Gazette.*

FIAMMETTA. A SUMMER IDYL. By W. W. STORY, Author of 'Roba di Roma,' 'Graffiti d'Italia,' &c. Crown 8vo, 7s. 6d.

THE ROYAL MAIL. ITS CURIOSITIES AND ROMANCE. By JAMES WILSON HYDE, Superintendent in the General Post-Office, Edinburgh. New Edition, Enlarged. With numerous Illus-trations. Crown 8vo, 6s.

"The whole of the volume is so full of fascination that, once taken up, it is difficult to lay it down."—*Times.*

"An extremely readable and meritorious book."—*St James's Gazette.*

"This volume is a storehouse of amusing anecdotes."—*Pall Mall Gazette.*

FROM KORTI TO KHARTUM: A JOURNAL OF THE DESERT MARCH FROM KORTI TO GUBAT, AND OF THE ASCENT OF THE NILE IN GENERAL GORDON'S STEAMERS. By COLONEL SIR CHARLES W. WILSON, K.C.B., K.C.M.G., R.E., &c.; late Deputy Adjutant-General (Intelligence Branch), Nile Expedi-tion. Third Edition. Crown 8vo, with Maps and Plans. 7s. 6d.

ALTIORA PETO. By LAURENCE OLIPHANT, Author of 'Piccadilly,' 'Traits and Travesties,' &c. Seventh Edition, with Illustrations, crown 8vo, 6s.

"Brilliant and delightful.......The book is one which every one will read and greatly admire.......It contains enough to equip a score of ordinary novelists for the production of a score of extraordinary novels."—*Athenæum.*

"May be characterised as a novel of a thousand, if only for the fact that it may be read through consecutively twice, or even thrice, with augmented pleasure to the reader with every fresh perusal.......It is not as a story that 'Altiora Peto' challenges warm admiration, but as a brilliant picture of life and manners."—*Spectator.*

New and Cheaper Edition.

GEORGE ELIOT'S LIFE. AS RELATED IN HER LETTERS AND JOURNALS. Arranged and Edited by her Husband, J. W. CROSS. With Portraits and other Illustrations. CABINET EDITION, with Additional Matter. Three Volumes, crown 8vo, 15s.

NOVELS BY GEORGE ELIOT. Cheaper Editions. Crown 8vo, with Illustrations. Viz. :—

ADAM BEDE, 3s. 6d.—THE MILL ON THE FLOSS. 3s. 6d.—FELIX HOLT, THE RADICAL, 3s. 6d.—SCENES OF CLERICAL LIFE, 3s.—SILAS MARNER, 2s. 6d.—ROMOLA, with Vignette, 3s. 6d.—DANIEL DERONDA, with Vignette, 7s. 6d.—MIDDLEMARCH, with Vignette, 7s. 6d.

NOVELS BY LAURENCE W. M. LOCKHART. New Uniform Edition in Three Volumes, crown 8vo, 6s. each.

I. DOUBLES AND QUITS.—II. FAIR TO SEE.—III. MINE IS THINE.

THE PRINCIPLES OF SINGING. A PRACTICAL GUIDE FOR VOCALISTS AND TEACHERS. With Vocal Exercises. By ALBERT B. BACH, Author of 'On Musical Education and Vocal Culture.' Crown 8vo, 6s.

"A work whose value is unquestionable. It would be quite possible to write at length in praise of the work, especially of the excellent musical examples, and to commend its excellence in detail, but the principles are set forward so clearly and agreeably, that it is not necessary to do more than heartily recommend all who are interested in the subject to buy the book and master its contents for themselves."—*Morning Post.*

THE WHITE ANGEL OF THE POLLY ANN, AND OTHER STORIES. A Book of Fables and Fancies. By J. LOGIE ROBERTSON, M.A., Author of 'Orellana, and other Poems.' Fcap. 8vo, 3s. 6d.

"There is greater exuberance of fresh and sparkling imagination, more narrative grace and quiet sunny humour, than in many a book ten times its bulk. ......The book is one from which old readers, as well as young ones, may derive both pleasure and profit."—*Scotsman.*

WILLIAM BLACKWOOD & SONS, EDINBURGH AND LONDON.

www.ingramcontent.com/pod-product-compliance
Lightning Source LLC
Chambersburg PA
CBHW030620030726
47497CB00006B/1578